THE UNREAL DANCE

SOUDABEH MACCLANCY

For Chloe, Izzadora and Tobias

For all those who've passed through my life....

The conversation still goes on.

The Unreal Dance
First edition: July, 2025

Shadowed Dance Publications
© 2025 Soudabeh Macclancy
All rights reserved.

Printed in the United Kingdom
ISBN: 9798289463845

With the deepest of gratitude for Vicks, JC, Strummer and Jones.

Deep into that dawn I go,
Not light---but an edge of darkness.

And when the shadows clear,
I see not truth,
But a bleak and unreal dance.

I have heard it said that the pattern of life, in a great many respects, mirrors that of the opera.

ACT I Love and Passion

ACT II Lies and Betrayal

ACT III Tragedy and Death

How true. How very true.

PROLOGUE

I speak but no-one hears me.
I shout but there is no response.
I scream--- only to be met by a dense silence.

I feel like a sleepwalker in my own life.
I am in a prison of my own making.
The rooms of my new flat are large and high-ceilinged, yet I feel a sense of suffocation.
The tall windows that face the sea do not look out onto the world---but inward staring into the dark void that is now my life.
There is nothing here to remind me of my past life.
No books, no ornaments, no photographs.

It is strange how we all collect these things to remind us of certain moments in our lives. They are like book-marks separating the different chapters.
Photographs are usually a reminder of a sunnier place, a happier time.
Grief and misery need no reminders. They come in frames of their own.
One knows, with a piercing sharpness, what has gone on before and what comes after.
The timing, the end of the story, gives a changed meaning to what has preceded it.

ACT I
LOVE AND PASSION

And the Lord shall smite thee,
With madness and blindness,
And astonishment of the heart.

1

Stella took a sip of her coffee and carried on staring out of the window. The garden, in the square below, was deserted. It was still quite early. Adam had already left---saying that he might be home a little earlier than usual.

The day stretched in front of her. Stella loved Mondays. It was a day she tried hard to keep to herself. Although she never planned anything ahead, there was a pattern.

She always ended up at one of two restaurants. Her choice depended on the weather. If it was dry she would take the longer walk to the Turkish restaurant and, if it was raining, she would go to the small Polish restaurant. Both were quiet at lunch time. She always sat at the same table in each place---and nearly always ordered the same meal. The day was clear and sunny. She would take the longer route.

Stella poured herself a second cup of coffee and sat down at the dining-room table. She started to make a list of things to be done—but then decided against it. After lunch she would stop at the Greek delicatessen, to put together a picnic for supper. She would then spend the next couple of hours looking through the book shops on her way home. Finally, she would stop at the flower shop to pick her usual order. Dark purple freesias and creamy, pale pink roses.

She looked at the clock. It was ten minutes to nine. Mrs. Hughes, the cleaning lady, would be here at any moment. She smiled to herself. She had never had a cleaning lady before moving here.

Stella had lived here for almost a year—but she had still not gotten used to the beauty of the spacious high-ceilinged rooms.

The flat had three large bedrooms. Adam used one as his office and suggested that she take the spare room as somewhere for her to work. When she had said that she really did not need that amount of space, he had replied that everyone needed a corner of their own. A place that afforded some sort of privacy.

Stella would soon become acquainted with the fine line between privacy and secrecy.

A key sounded in the door. It was Mrs Hughes. Stella went to the kitchen to get her a cup of coffee. She reminded her that the laundry would be collected later that day and that there was a delivery due before twelve o'clock. This would have to be signed for. She then went to take a shower and get dressed.

After her shower Stella put on a pair of jeans and a dark blue jumper of Adam's. The jumper was far too large on her—but the familiar scent of him gave her a sense of comfort, of safety. These were words that often came into her mind when she thought of him. These were things that she needed. She did not crave the drama and excitement of a roller-coaster life. She could only give herself fully in the knowledge of there being a strong safety-net, a strong structure.

Stella went into the room that she now used as an office. She sat down at the desk that faced the window. She was aware of the sounds of the washing machine and the dishwasher. She could hear Mrs. Hughes' tuneless humming, as she worked her way through the flat with the vacuum cleaner. She could smell the furniture polish mixed with the scent of flowers. She felt an overwhelming sense of happiness. If only one could realize, at that given time, how precious these moments truly were. So as not to squander them so carelessly.

The desk that Stella sat at was large, with a set of drawers at each end. The left-hand wall housed floor to ceiling bookshelves. The wall on the right was covered by a framed green baize notice board. This was to display the various invitations to the fund-raising events that she had to attend. Stella worked as a consultant for a company that organized these for a number of charities.

She loved this room. Living with Adam was still quite new to her. And he was right---everyone needed a private place, a place to retreat to. How little did she realize, at the time, how much she would need this space. How she would soon look on it not as a place to retreat to---but rather as a place to hide in. It would, in time, become her shelter.

She looked down at her desk. It was almost bare. A slim laptop computer, a round glass vase of roses, a large pad of lined paper and a small tray containing at least a dozen pens. These pens were from the hotels she had stayed at, the restaurants she had eaten in, the conferences she had attended.

They were a record of her life over the past few months. Where she had stayed, what she had eaten, people she had met. It's funny how something as insignificant as a pen could harbour so many memories. All locked into a plastic tube. The password being whatever word is printed on it.

Stella raised her head and stared out of the window. The day was clear with a low blinding sun. The blossoms were coming out on the trees, this giving the day a sense of hope. On days like these one thinks of life, of fate, of opportunities taken and those missed. Of course, there are no answers or conclusions. It is just a gentle process of enquiry.

Her mind was on Adam. She thought back to when they had first met. It was at a Christmas party given by one of the national newspapers. The party was being held on the first floor of a London club. Stella had arrived rather later than she had hoped to. The room was already full and the noise of the various conversations, all taking place at the same time, was quite deafening.
She managed to get herself a drink. She then looked around and saw a small space at the other end of the room where she could safely stand without being jostled.

When she got there, she leaned against the wall and took a look around the room to see if there was anyone there that she recognized. There were a few people that she knew, through work, but she was too tired to move through the crowds. She would finish her drink first; say hello to those she knew and then try and leave as soon as possible after that. She really longed for an early night.

As Stella turned to put down her glass on a small table next to her, she noticed someone standing beside her. She felt him being there, rather than saw him. She made a move to get past him, but he laid a hand on her arm to stop her. He told her that on no account was she to give up the best place in the room and that, if she would stay where she was, he would be brave enough to go and get her another drink. She smiled and nodded her head.

When he returned, carrying their drinks, they introduced themselves. Stella, Adam. Adam, Stella.

The noise in the room made any attempts at conversation all but impossible.

Adam suggested that they would be more comfortable in the bar downstairs.

This was almost as noisy, but at least they managed to find a table to sit at.

To this day Stella could not remember exactly what they had talked about.

He had asked about her work, asking intelligent and pertinent questions.

When she asked him about his work, she noticed that his whole manner changed. He became animated and talked with a passion that belied his otherwise calm and reserved demeanour.

Adam worked as a journalist on a weekly news magazine. He specialized in analysing the political and economic patterns that could precipitate unrest in fast emerging economies.

While he talked, she watched his face. He was both articulate and passionate.

He spoke to her as if she were as familiar with his subject as he was. Stella felt flattered.

It was getting late—but she no longer felt tired. When Adam suggested that they should go on somewhere to eat she did not even hesitate.

The restaurant was a ten-minute walk away. It was a small family run place, warm and welcoming.

The owner seemed to know Adam well and after a few exchanges, he showed
them to a corner table.

Stella found herself sitting in a restaurant that she had never been to, with a man that she had only met a few hours before. And yet she felt an overwhelming sense of the familiar. She had no doubts that she was meant to be sitting at this particular table, with this particular man, on this particular night. It was as if she was continuing a conversation that had begun a long, long while ago.

The Unreal Dance

Even now she could not remember what they had eaten, what they had drunk or what they had talked about. When she thought back to that evening all she could really remember was a feeling of warmth, a feeling of belonging, a feeling of not being on the outside looking in.

Looking back to that evening, Stella wondered if everyone was possessed of a self-destructive side. She thought of what would lead her to so carelessly throw away something so precious. Something she had been looking for, for so long. Perhaps it is human nature to constantly challenge the jealous Gods.
In most instances it is an uneven battle.

They left the restaurant and walked for a while in silence. They were both oblivious to the lateness of the hour.

Finally, Adam hailed a taxi, saying that he would first take her home, then go on from there. As it turned out they did not live far from each other—only a short walk away. But Adam already knew this. Stella may never have noticed him, but he knew a great deal about her.

When Adam had paid the taxi, he walked her to her door. He stood looking at her in silence for a while. He then kissed her lightly on the forehead and said that he would be in touch. He turned to her briefly as he walked away, he then seemed to melt into the dark.

When Stella went to sleep that night, it was to dream of sitting on a wooden bench in a large garden, crowded with scented flowers and flitting butterflies.
Beside her on the bench was someone whose face she could not see. He had his arm around her, his chin resting on the top of her head. When she awoke, she could still remember the warmth of the sun on her face, and the heat of his body against hers.

Adam did not call her for a couple of weeks. In fact, it was just before the New Year. Stella often took out the piece of paper he had given her, with his telephone number on it. But she did not call. Rather, she embraced the anticipation of the wait, certain in the knowledge that they would see each other again.

When he did call, toward the end of December, the conversation was brief.

He asked Stella if she would like to see in the New Year with him. She said she would.

And that was how it started. There was no drama nor any hesitation between them. Being together seemed to be the natural order of things. Stella did not mind his long working hours nor his assignments abroad, and he did not mind her silences and her need for privacy.

She looked at her watch. She would have to leave soon. Before leaving she went over to the notice board to check on the list of events that were coming up over the next few weeks. It was then that she saw a card and a handwritten note, from Adam, pinned to the bottom left-hand side of the board. Stella looked at the card and the note for several minutes, hesitating before reaching out to take them.

Looking back, she often wondered whether in those moments she had had some sort of premonition about what was to unfold. She was not the sort of person to harbour fanciful thoughts, but the events that would follow made her visit and revisit those few minutes, searching for any clue.

Stella reached out, taking the card and the note. The card was an invitation to a showing of paintings, drawings and sculptures by someone called Edward Falconer. Although she was not familiar with his work, she had heard of him. The gallery, in central London, was certainly a prestigious one. The works were titled 'Echoes from The Wilderness', a title she would remember for years to come.

Adam's note was just to ask her to keep the date of the opening free. He explained that Edward was a close friend of his. They had known each other since their school days. The date was some weeks away. She marked it in her diary.

Having taken her coat and bag from the hall cupboard, Stella said goodbye to Mrs. Hughes and made her way into the piercing sunshine.

She looked at her watch. She had plenty of time. She would take the longer route through the side streets and then make her way across the park. All the uneasiness that she had felt earlier had left her. She had a sense of peace. There was an order about her life with Adam. There was not that state of chaos that seemed to be constantly present in others' lives.

As a child, and even now, Stella would pick flowers, drying them between the pages of an exercise book or a diary, the sap making them stick to the pages. Months, or even years later, when she came across them again, she would remember a time or a place. The memories were sometimes exact and, at other times, not unlike faded photographs. And like a chain, the memories would, in some way, become linked. But at the time they each appeared as a complete image, each in its own frame.

She came to a small antique shop that specialised in glass. In the past Stella would often stop here. In the far corner of the shop there was a cabinet, housing the most exquisite collection of glass perfume bottles. The bottles ranged from plain glass to pale greens, to peacock blues, to deep pinks and reds. The cabinet was a glass dome, lit from inside. It rotated slowly and each time that the same bottle would pass it would look slightly different. If you half closed your eyes, you could imagine the various dressing tables each had sat on, and the various hands each had been held by.

This was where Stella would come to buy presents for her mother. Her mother had died some years before but, entering the shop, memories of her
came back with a sharp focus. Although she often had difficulty in picturing her face, she could still smell the scent of her perfume and feel herself being held against the silk of her clothes. These were memories that seemed not to fade or distort. And she would jealously guard these, not allowing the passing of time to steal them from her.

She was about to go in and have a look around when she remembered that Adam was coming home earlier than usual. She started to walk faster and headed towards the park. There would be time to return another day.

How strange that even as adults we count on the continuity and pattern of our lives with the certainty of that of a child. But to think any differently might weave fear into every strand of our actions. It would be a life not fully lived.

And yet, for so long to come, Stella would feel with deep regret her decision not to enter the shop that day.

She made her way toward the park, not stopping to look into any of the small shops that she usually looked into.

Stella cut diagonally across the park, making her way to the large pond at the centre. Here she watched two children, a boy and a girl, manoeuvring an old-fashioned model sailing boat. The hull was beautifully polished, and the sails had been newly washed. They each took it in turns to hold the long rod that would allow the boat to move across the water. She watched their faces.

Their faces furrowed with concentration and absorption---oblivious to anything that might be going on around them.

She stood looking on for some time. She had never really considered having any children of her own. There had never been a time in her life that had provided the level of stability needed. But now things had changed. And fanciful as it seemed, she started to consider the possibility. It was as if a germ had been planted.

Although Stella and Adam had lived together for almost a year the subject of children had never come up. This was to stay on her mind for the rest of the day.

She finished making her way across the park and crossing a main road, she reached the small road that would lead her to the Turkish restaurant.

When Stella arrived, she was astonished to find that the place was almost full. She had become accustomed to the quiet of a Monday lunchtime. Hassan, the owner, made his way over to her and guided her to a small table at the back. He went to the bar and returned with a glass of wine and the menu. He knew that she never looked at the menu---always ordering the same dish. She smiled at him and ordered her usual meal. He smiled back. Over the years this had become something of a private joke between them.

Her food arrived and she set about carefully shelling the large prawns and dipping them into the garlic and lemon butter. She ordered a second glass of wine and sat thinking back to the two children in the park. It was as if she was visiting a territory she had never explored before. There was excitement and a little fear.

Stella paid her bill and made her way through the dim light of the restaurant into the blinding sunshine of the street. She found herself smiling.

She crossed the road and took the small side street that led to the Greek delicatessen. Here she stood still for a few minutes before deciding what to choose. There were jars of the plump green queen olives and those of the more delicate black Kalamata ones. There was the smell of freshly baked bread and the scent of the thyme and rosemary roast potatoes.

Stella put together a picnic of stuffed vine leaves, spiced meatballs, bread, olives and a selection of sweet pastries dripping with honey.

Looking at her watch she realized that she would have to take a taxi home.

She had spent too long in the park on her way here. She would stop at the flower shop to pick up her order.

When Stella let herself into the flat, she noticed that the delivery that she had been waiting for had arrived. She took the food and the flowers into the kitchen and collected a sharp knife to open the package with. Having carefully removed all the wrapping she stood back and looked at the large, beautifully carved wooden box. In the centre of the carvings there was an elephant inlaid in mother-of-pearl. Inside, the box was divided into sections. There was a place that would hold pens and ones that would house smaller objects. She had seen it in an antique shop some while ago. She had immediately thought of it for Adam. It would sit on his desk.

After she had arranged the flowers, Stella laid out the food and put the bread into the oven, ready to warm up at the last minute.

She walked slowly from room to room. She would occasionally touch an object or pick up a book. She never tired of doing this. She had not, as yet, got over the novelty of her new life. Each day it would fill her with a sense of wonder and anticipation.

When Stella had first moved in with Adam there had been casual dinners held for friends. There had been people dropping in for drinks. But gradually, as if by some silent and secret agreement between them, these occasions had become quite rare. They wanted to be on their own. Even when they were attending a function, or at a party, they had developed a way of quietly signalling, one to the other, that they would like to leave. Their home had become a haven for them both. But the walls that one builds with such love and attention can just as quickly come down---leaving one exposed and vulnerable.

Stella picked a bud from one of the freesias and put it in the box she had bought for Adam. She placed the box on his desk. He would see it later.

She heard the sound of his key in the door. She smiled to herself and went to greet him. She had been looking forward to seeing him all day.

When they had finished their supper, Adam went into his study to look through his mail. Stella, unseen, quietly watched him from the doorway. He was sitting looking at the box. He opened the top and took out the flower bud. He smelled it and returned it to its place. She moved away.

A few minutes later she felt him standing behind her. He turned her around and wrapped her in his arms. They stood like that for some time. He then gently kissed her on the top of her head.

'Thank you', he said, 'thank you'.

Adam returned to his study to finish off some work. He said that he would not be long.

Stella picked up a book and curled herself deep into the corner of the sofa. She loved this time of day when Adam was home. She could hear him moving around, occasionally making a telephone call. When he had finished working, he would come and sit with her. They would discuss their plans for the days and, sometimes, for the weeks ahead. They would sit and watch the television or just sit and read. Finding that she could not concentrate on her book, Stella sat looking out through the darkened windows to the lights on the square. She looked at the windows on the opposite side. Although it was not late, many had drawn curtains and lowered blinds. The others were not unlike the split screens that one would see on the television. The bright lights of a kitchen, the more mellow lighting of a sitting-room. People moving around---as in a silent film. Meals being eaten, conversations being had. She often wondered if they ever watched her.

When Adam had finished, he suggested that they should go out for a walk. The evening was cold but clear. They took their usual route. They went around the square and up a long side street. Here they entered a small bar. It was dimly lit and warm. They found a quiet table towards the back. Adam ordered two coffees and two brandies.

'Did you see the note I left you this morning?', he asked.
'I did. I've put it in the diary. I had no idea that you knew Edward Falconer. I have heard of him but I'm not familiar with his work.'

The Unreal Dance

Adam explained that he and Edward had been friends since their schooldays. It was a friendship that had endured, over the years, in spite of the long absences, both on his part and on Edward's. And although they sometimes only managed to meet once or twice a year, their conversation would take up where it had last left off. It was a friendship based on a deep mutual liking and a deep mutual trust. This last was a statement that Stella would think back to, again and again, over the years to come.

"Edward is a complex man,' Adam said. 'A mixture of intensity and humour. Of passion and silence. At times I feel as if I barely know him. At other times I feel that there are few people that I am so close to. He comes from a quite strange family. The large house and the elaborate grounds seem to act as a backdrop to an intricate and disturbing drama. On the occasions that I have met them they all appeared, in some peculiar way, to be acting out a well-rehearsed play. His father is not unlike a caricature of a country squire and his mother a cold and rather distant creature. He has a sister, Grace. I've only met her twice. Edward rarely refers to her.'

Stella listened in silence. She took a sip of her brandy, her coffee having long gone cold. This was a story she could feel herself being drawn into.

'At first', Adam continued, 'I was fascinated by all of it. Edward's parents, the house, the way they lived. It was so different to anything that I was used to. But then, gradually, I started to feel a sense of claustrophobia. A lack of warmth, as if they were all disconnected. After we both left school, I stopped going there.'

Having paid the bill, Adam helped Stella on with her coat and taking her hand they went out into the night.

They said little on the way back to the flat. Adam's mind was on a meeting he had the next day and Stella's mind was on the story that he had just recounted to her. And then her mind went back to her walk through the park earlier that day. Of the two children guiding their model boat over the pond and of the look of concentration on their young faces. The image had stayed deeply etched in her memory.

As they let themselves into the flat, they heard the sound of the telephone ringing. It was the telephone in Adam's office. He took the call, which lasted some twenty minutes or more. When he had finished, he came into the kitchen where Stella was putting away a few dishes.

'That was my editor. He wants me to go out to Hong Kong. There has been an ongoing investigation into the affairs of one of the large investment banks, and it appears that there are some very serious irregularities. He wants me to go out to cover the story. I'll be gone for at least a week---maybe more. I'm really sorry. I know we had plans for this weekend. I'll make it up to you. I'll take a few days off when I get back.'

Stella went over to him, putting her arms around him and laying her head on his chest.

'Perhaps we can take the trip we've always been fantasizing about. The one on a bleak coastline. Where we can tuck ourselves away in a small hotel, with roaring fires inside and howling gales outside.'

Adam laughed. They had been talking about this trip from almost the day they had met.

Turning all the lights off, they went to bed. Adam would need an early start.

That night Stella dreamt about the park. Only in the dream there were not just the two children that she had been watching earlier. There were dozens of them. Each with their own small boat. All the hulls were newly varnished and all the sails newly washed. As she approached them, they all turned around at the same time. Their faces were exact, miniature replicas of Adam's face.

When Stella awoke the next morning, Adam had already left. She found a note on the kitchen table---saying that he had gone to the office and that he would call her before flying out. She felt a strange sense of emptiness, which was rather unusual for her. It was as if they started an important conversation that they had not had time to finish. She then remembered her dream and all the little faces.

2

Adam got up in the early hours of the morning. Having packed the night before, he just had to sort out the paperwork that he needed to take with him. He went about this as quietly as he could so as not to wake Stella. He went back into the bedroom and stood for some while, watching her in her sleep.

Even in her sleep she had an air of neatness and self-containment. She lay curled up on her side with both hands placed under her left cheek. He desperately wanted to wake her, to say goodbye, but decided against it. Instead, he left her a note on the kitchen table. He would miss her. He went down to his waiting taxi. It was not yet quite light, but just enough so that you knew you were leaving the dark country of the night toward the arrival of the day.

On the journey Adam stared sightlessly out of the window. He thought about how his life had changed and smiled, to himself, in anticipation of the time to come. This feeling of contentment was new to him.

After his meeting, and having checked in at the airport, Adam called Stella.

'You should have woken me,' she said.

'I couldn't. That would have been unkind. You looked as if you were dreaming the dream of the Gods. I wanted you to reach the end of it. Take great care darling. I'll call you when I arrive.'

On the flight Adam found that he could not concentrate on his work. This was unusual for him. In the past he had had no difficulty focusing his attention on the task in hand. Instead, he found his mind going back to the first time he had seen Stella. It was about eighteen months before the Christmas party where they had actually met.

He was attending a fundraising event for a charitable foundation. The party was being held in a large glass and steel art gallery, in a central London park. It was a summer's evening---the edge of the warmth taken off by a light breeze. Adam did not intend to stay long. He had just returned from a long assignment in the Far East and was looking forward to some time on his own. He picked up a drink and made his way through one of the gallery areas, toward a friend of his who was involved in the organizing of this event. As he had almost reached her, he saw Stella. He suddenly felt as if he had been rooted to the spot. He stood, drink in hand, looking at her for several minutes before he could even make himself move. He then made his way toward Anna, whose invitation had first brought him here.

When he finally reached Anna, she was deep in conversation with one of the guests. She smiled at him and indicated that she would be with him shortly. He took this time to look around to see if he could find Stella again. After a few moments he found her. She was standing, only a short way away, talking to a small group of people. And even though she was smiling and seemed to be explaining something to one of the group, she appeared to be, in some way, completely apart. There was a stillness and quietness about her that suggested that she was only going through the motions of socializing, that perhaps she had acquired a way of meeting the outside world, without totally taking part.

Adam suddenly noticed that Anna was standing beside him, watching him with some amusement.

'Adam', she remarked, 'you seem to be entirely captivated'.
He slowly turned to her, but did not reply.

'That's Stella', she said. 'She works as a consultant for arranging events for various charities. She's good. She's very good. Clever and creative with her ideas. We've worked on several projects, together, over the past three or four years. We've developed a good working relationship, a friendship even. But I often feel that I've got as close to her as she'll allow me. There is a side to her that is quite unfathomable. A barrier that she seems not to want to let down. It's not, I think, that she's secretive. It's more that she has a strong sense of privacy---a need to establish trust first. Would you like me to introduce you to her?'

'No. But thank you. I feel that this may not be the right time. I have absolutely no doubt that the right time will come.'

The Unreal Dance

Having said goodbye, Adam glanced briefly in Stella's direction, before leaving. He thought about her a great deal that evening, wondering what it was about her that he had felt so drawn to.

Weeks passed. And months passed. He attended any charity events that he could---in the hope of running into Stella. But all his attempts turned out to be fruitless. That was until almost a year later. He was coming out of a side street near his flat, when he saw her. Adam, doing something so out of character for him, started to follow her. She went into a small Italian delicatessen and came out about ten minutes later, carrying a package. She then went into the newsagent's, coming out carrying several magazines. He then followed her to a block of flats, not far from his own. She took out a key and let herself in. He had finally found her---living within a short walking distance, from where he, himself, lived. This was really quite unbelievable. He stood there for a few moments, then went home. He felt like buying every tabloid newspaper he could find and reading his horoscope. But he drew the line at that.

After that, Adam would keep walking past her block of flats, hoping to catch a glimpse of her. But he did not, not until that December when they finally met.

Adam thought back over the past year. His life with Stella had given him a sense of peace. A backdrop for a future that held so much promise. There had been many women in his life. Some of these affairs had been short lived, and some had lasted a great deal longer. But none of them seemed to show much substance. In life, he had found that he had never known what he was looking for. He only knew when he had found it. And this time he was certain that he had found it.

Adam's thoughts then turned to Edward. He compared his own settled life with that of Edward's always chaotic one.

He remembered their time at school. They had become close friends--- but it was a strange and unlikely friendship. Edward, so clever and so charismatic. He seemed to excel at everything. He achieved so much, outwardly making it all appear effortless. Adam was quiet and reserved, slowly moving in Edward's shadow. Edward was always going to be the prize-winner. Adam had acknowledged this from early on and had never resented him for it.

Then toward the end of their school days there had been tragedy in Edward's family. Edward had an older sister, Grace. They were extremely close. Almost uncomfortably so. They were like a secret society of two. Inseparable. Then Angela, Edward's mother, had given birth to another daughter, Lily. From the first, Edward had become quite besotted with her. It was as if Lily was his own child. He would spend hours with her, helping her when she took her first steps, reading to her, even when she was too young to understand. During the school holidays Adam rarely saw him. He was completely absorbed in the young child. Grace's resentment became obvious to everyone but Edward. She became more and more withdrawn. Her parents just assumed that she was going through a difficult phase, seemingly oblivious, as was Edward, to her apparent pain.

When the child was almost four, Edward, out of his own savings, bought her a black Labrador puppy. Lily named the dog Ted, her name for Edward. He was both flattered and amused. The three of them became inseparable. They could be seen playing in the grounds, often going down to the large pond, where Lily would feed the ducks, Edward keeping a watchful eye on her.

It was here that she and the puppy were found a few weeks later, both drowned in the pond. It was late afternoon. Edward was in his room studying for the end of term exams. The child became impatient and wanted to go out to play. Grace had offered to take her. Later, a tearful Grace said that she had only run back to the house for a few minutes. She had had to use the toilet, and she had been unable to persuade Lily to go with her. There was a verdict of accidental drowning.

Edward was inconsolable. He withdrew from all social activities, instead immersing himself in his schoolwork. Adam saw little of him after this. Even in later years when they would meet up for the occasional drink, or dinner, he never referred to this incident. Neither did he ever speak of Grace.

One day, after some time had elapsed after their last meeting, Edward telephoned, asking Adam if they could meet for dinner. Adam was delighted. He had been watching, with great interest and pride, Edward's career as a painter and sculptor. They arranged to meet the following week. There had been a sense of urgency in Edward's voice.

When they met, Adam was astonished at Edward's news. He said that he was getting married in a month's time and that he wanted Adam to be his best man. Edward had always maintained that the trappings of marriage and children were not for him. There was no place in his life for either.

'You see', Edward said,' even after all these years, you're still the person I'm closest to.'

'I'm flattered. And of course I'll be there.'

Edward did not mention the subject of his marriage again. Instead, he asked Adam about his work and told him about his.

A few days later Adam left for an assignment in the Middle East and did not see, or talk to Edward, until the eve of his wedding. Still, Edward said nothing about the woman he was marrying, other than her name was Lydia.

The wedding took place in a register office at 11 o'clock the next morning.
The reception was being held at a restaurant nearby. Edward had not, much to his parents' dismay, wanted it to be held at the house. The memories of that place still, after so many years, casting a long and enveloping shadow.

When Adam first saw Lydia, he was completely taken aback. She was so different to any other of the women he had seen Edward with. They had been both striking and confident. They had an air of worldliness. Lydia was a total contrast. She was pretty, rather than beautiful. She looked shy, reserved and a little frightened. There was a fragility about her. And a haunted look in her eyes---almost as if she could foresee the way that the story would unfold.

The wedding reception was a small one. A few of Edward's London friends, and a few of his family. Grace was absent. Lydia's parents stood alone at the back, looking perplexed at finding themselves in this rather colourful gathering.

Having spoken briefly to Edward's parents, Adam went over to Lydia, to introduce himself.

'I'm so pleased to finally meet you', she said, her smile lighting up her face. 'Edward often talks about you. He makes your earlier years sound not unlike a Boys' Own story.'

'And I'm delighted to meet you. Don't take too much notice of Edward's tales. His imagination can be extremely creative. I think that everyone is waiting for my speech. You'll find my version of the past somewhat closer to reality.'

That was to be the last time Adam saw or spoke to Lydia again. She and Edward had left the reception, unseen, a short while later.

A little more than a year later, the marriage had broken down. Adam was to find out the reasons a long while after.

His mind then went back to Stella. He tried to picture what she would be doing at this exact moment. She would be either in the kitchen or in her study. This gave him a sense of comfort. When he thought of her, he could imagine a future. Something that he had not been able to do before. His past relationships had all seemed to come with a start and a finish. He had a certainty about this one. Before falling asleep, he remembered thinking that he would take Stella to meet his parents, on his return. It was time.

3

When Adam had called from the airport, Stella was making coffee. The smell mingled with that of wood polish and the heady perfume of the flowers. The light was streaming in from the windows. The French windows to the balcony were open---the morning air bringing in, with it, the scent of new mown grass, from the square below. She picked up the telephone after the first ring. She instinctively knew it was him. Their conversation did not last long. But afterward, she thought back to it. She plucked out the word 'darling'. She held onto it. Neither she, nor Adam, were given to using endearments. Rather, they conveyed their feelings through a touch or a glance. She felt as if she had been handed a precious gift.

There was a part of her life that Stella had kept to herself. The emotions that she felt, even now, even after all these years still arose like bile, in her throat. The only person that had known, the only person that she had been able to talk to about it, had been her mother. And now she was gone. The death of her mother had left her in a dark void, a no-man's land that she found difficult to navigate. With the passing of the years, she wished that she could have confided in someone else, as well as her mother. She had close friends, but she had been too ashamed to let them see her weakness, to let them see her fear. And, at the time, she was afraid that they would not believe her. She had worked long and hard to preserve the perfect facade. All they would see was what she had chosen to present to them. And now it was too late to try and explain the extent of the hurt and the pain that she had suffered. The humiliation, the loss of self-belief, an enduring mistrust of the outside world. These were not things that would be overcome easily.

Before setting up her own consultancy, Stella had worked in an advertising agency. The clients were mostly from film and television companies. The work was hard, and the clients were, for the most part, quite difficult. She was good at organizing. She was able to take the sting out of most of the dramas and to level the chaos. She worked hard and put in long hours. Soon she was to head one of the smaller accounts. A company based in central London. Most of their work was in producing in-house commercials for the larger corporations. But they had gained a reputation for making rather outstanding low budget films. They were attracting a great deal of attention both here and overseas. That was where she met Jack. He was one of the partners in the film company. He was the man who would cast a long shadow over the rest of her life.

From the start Jack was attentive. Stella had arrived at the offices of the film studios feeling both nervous and apprehensive. This was the first time that she would be heading her own account. There was a small team of people, from the agency, that would be assisting her, but the direction taken, and the decisions taken, would largely be hers. Jack was aware of her fears and from the beginning, took great pains to make her feel at ease.

'You mustn't be afraid', he had said, 'here we work as a team. And you are now part of that team. We're here to help you and give you all the support that you might need.'

'I'll do my best', she had replied. 'And thank you.'

'Just keep remembering that you were given this account because you were the best person for it. There will be difficult times, and the occasional heated argument. But please don't take it personally. It's what happens when you put
a group of creative people together around a table.'

With that he went back to his office. He had introduced Stella to his assistant, saying that she would show her around and acquaint her with the other members of the team.

This, and the looking over of the ideas for future projects, took the best part of the day. Stella felt overwhelmed. She went back to the agency. She worked until late. Tomorrow would be the first proper meeting. She had to be well prepared.

She reached the studios half an hour earlier than the meeting was to take place. Jack was there to greet her.

'I knew you would arrive early', he laughed. 'Your reputation as a hard worker has gone before you. I've arranged for you to have your own office. And please don't hesitate to ask for anything that you might need. I'd like you to come and go freely. The studios open early and don't close until late. Quite often, if we are nearing the end of a project, they don't close at all.'

The meeting started at 9 o'clock. Everyone welcomed Stella and hoped that she would enjoy working with them. The initial discussions were focused on budgets, schedules and timelines. These were areas that she was not familiar with and would have to be looked at, in greater detail, later. At lunchtime sandwiches were brought in and they took a half hour break. The afternoon session centred around marketing and promotion. This was Stella's field. She listened with great care, occasionally putting forward a tentative suggestion. Each time that she did this, Jack would note down any comments that she had made, often praising her for her ideas and her quick grasp of the situation in hand. She felt both flattered and grateful. She was to later remember that the relationship between them, that followed, would be largely based on gratitude. Hers, not his.

Stella divided her time between her office, at the studios, and her office at the agency. Often, she would return to the film studios, working till a late hour.

It was here that Jack found her one night. She did not notice him at first. She was completely absorbed in a report that had to be ready for the next day. She became aware of him when he gently placed a hand on her shoulder.

'It's time to stop, Stella. I'm going to take you out for a drink then put you in a taxi home.'

She smiled. She could do with a drink.

They went to a nearby brasserie. Jack asked her if she would like something to eat. She said that just a drink would be fine.

Jack talked at length, about the work that he and his two partners were doing. The in-house commercials that they made, were to part-fund where their interests really lay. That of low budget films. Films that would be artistically good but would also carry a significant social message. His voice was hypnotic and his enthusiasm infectious. As she listened, Stella found herself becoming completely absorbed. She saw him look at his watch. It was late.

'Get a good night's sleep, Stella. Tomorrow's going to be a long day.'

The next day was a long day. So were the days that followed. And each night the two of them would go to the same bar, sit at the same table and order the same drinks. On each occasion Jack would look at his watch, at almost exactly the same time, and suggested they leave. He had never said where he was going on to. And Stella had never asked.

The weeks passed and the months passed. Their time together each night had become something of a ritual. Jack would talk and Stella would listen. Then, one night, he did not turn up. He had left the office without even saying goodbye to her. She waited, thinking that he might return. He did not. In fact, he did not come back to the office for two days. He missed appointments and meetings. No-one commented on this. She was later to learn that this was a pattern with him. A pattern, she later realized, that was to be an established part of her life with him. Looking back, she wished that she had placed more importance on this.

When he did come back, toward the end of the week, nothing was said between them. She was hurt and perplexed. She did not let it show.

A week after this incident, Jack came into her office. He asked if she would have dinner with him the next evening. He already seemed to know the answer. He said that he would let her know the arrangements the following morning.

The restaurant, where he had arranged they should meet, was not far from her flat. Stella was early. He arrived exactly on time and made his way over to their table.

'I hope you realize that this is a 'proper' date', he said. 'It's about time, don't you think? I've been waiting for this for a long time.'

She too had been waiting a long time for this.

Halfway through the meal he stood up, leant over the table, cupped his hands around her face, and kissed her.

The Unreal Dance

When he had sat down, they carried on eating and talking as if nothing had happened. But something had. It was to have unimaginable consequences, for her, for years to come.

When they left the restaurant, Jack walked her home. He did not ask to come in. He placed his hands on her shoulders and looked at her intently for a few moments.

'Goodnight, Stella. I'll see you in the morning.' With that he walked away.

At work Jack appeared distracted, often not even acknowledging her presence. Everyone was working long hours. It was nearing the end of a major project. Although they would often meet for a meal at the end of the day, he seemed preoccupied most of the time. It was a long time before he touched her again.

Then one day he asked her to come to his house for dinner. He gave her the address. If he noticed her confusion, he said nothing.

Later that day Stella found herself standing outside a tall, elegant house, in a North London crescent. Jack immediately opened the front door, as if he had been waiting for the sound of her steps. He had.

'I thought we would eat here', he said. 'I'm a passable cook, I've been told. Sit down. I'll get you a drink.'

She watched him as he moved around the kitchen. He was totally relaxed. This was a side of Jack that she would never of imagined would have existed.

The dining-room was immediately off the kitchen. It was a long, simple room, with glass doors opening onto a small garden.

Jack carried the food in. Stella was still standing by the doors, looking out.

'I grow all my own fruit and vegetables', he said.

'Next you'll be telling me you can walk on water', she laughed.

'I used to be able to. I'm a little out of practice.'

When they sat down to eat, Stella found that she was no longer nervous. They did not talk a great deal while they were eating. The silences were comfortable. They had coffee and brandies in the garden. It was getting cooler. They went inside. It was late, she had to get home. She would ask Jack to telephone for a taxi.

Before she could ask, he was beside her, turning her to face him. He held her for a long time, resting his chin on her head. He said nothing. She felt as if there was something important, he was trying to make up his mind about. There was. He took her hand and, wordlessly, led her upstairs.

There was both passion and anger in Jack's lovemaking. She felt as if he was trying to drive out some unseen demon. She was to realize, some months later, that he was.

When she awoke in the morning, it was to find him standing beside the bed, holding out a cup of coffee to her. He sat down on the edge of the bed and brushed her hair off her face.

"Move in with me, Stella. Not tomorrow, not next week. Tonight. I need you here with me, to help save me from myself.'

That evening she collected the few things that she would need from her flat.
The rest would be collected at the weekend. This was to be the most unexpected chapter in her life, so far. She did not, at any time, stop to question what she was doing. That would come later.

The first few months were both exciting and happy for Stella. Jack was
attentive and generous with his time. She had never lived with a man before. She had no idea what to expect. It had all been so sudden. She had thought that it might take time for them both to adjust. But they were both at ease from the start. There were nights he would have to attend business dinners with clients. He would always call to say he was on his way home. Stella sat reading, curled up on the sofa, listening out for the sound of his taxi.

Then Jack started to change. It was not really noticeable at first. Stella put it down to the fact that he was working so hard. The studio had been given a contract for a series of management training films for an oil company. The clients were proving to be unreasonably difficult. He was becoming moody.

The companionable silences that they had shared had turned into uncomfortable ones. On the nights that he was going to be late, he would often forget to let her know. He always apologised afterwards. But the same thing would happen again. He was also becoming very critical of her. Both at work and at home. She remembered that, not long ago, she could do no wrong. All her feelings of contentment were being slowly replaced by uncertainty.

Then one night, when she was expecting him home for dinner, he did not appear. Stella waited up a long time, unable to either concentrate on reading or watching television. A little after midnight she went up to bed. Sleep would not come. She lay awake on her side, constantly looking at the bed-side clock. It was after five in the morning before Jack came home. She could hear him moving around downstairs. She listened to the noise of the kettle and the coffee being stirred into the pot. She listened to the sound of the running water, as he took a shower. She listened to the sound of him opening and closing cupboard doors in the dressing-room. She waited for him to come into the bedroom and offer her some sort of explanation. But he did not. The next sound that Stella heard was that of the front door closing. She felt emotionally paralyzed---too numb to even cry.

When Stella got to the studios, there was no sign of Jack. In fact, he did not turn up all day. Again, the missed meetings and the missed appointments. And again, no-one said anything. She noticed that his assistant was avoiding having any contact with her, but that could have just been in her imagination.

She left early, feeling drained and unable to concentrate on her work. In this state she was liable to make serious mistakes, and she could not afford to do that. She did not go home straight away. She wanted to feel part of the outside world---suddenly aware that her life with Jack was beginning to suffocate her. She would find somewhere to have lunch, then walk around for a little, before going home. Stella needed time to think. She still had her flat to go back to if things got any worse. The problem lay with her job. She had broken the unwritten, unspoken, but often alluded to, rule of not physically, or emotionally, engaging with a client. Now she understood why.

When she arrived home, she noticed that the front door was open. She could hear the beautiful, but mournful strains of Cavatina, the theme music to the film The Deer Hunter. A favourite of Jack's. As she entered the hallway, Stella noticed that every vase in the house must have been used----there were flowers everywhere. She found Jack in the kitchen arranging food on a large plate. She saw that the dining-room table had been set. The candles ready to be lit, the wine ready to be opened. A round glass vase, like a miniature goldfish bowl, was filled with pale yellow roses. They were from the garden. He must have spent most of the day here.

He came up to her, standing close, but not touching her. He looked hesitant, uncertain.

'This is me grovelling, Stella,' he said. 'This is me grovelling.'
She moved past him toward the stairs.
'I'll be down in a few minutes. We can talk then.'

But there was to be no talking. No explanations. Just Jack, using his effortless charm.

His love-making that night was almost brutal. Stella's whole body ached for days to come. Afterwards she had curled herself into a tight ball, spending a sleepless night, facing away from him in the bed. The next morning, she saw that there was deep bruising on her inner thighs and her breasts. She thought that these bruises might serve as a reminder for the future. But they didn't. They would match the vicious verbal attacks that were to follow. Each time he was contrite. And each time she was to lose a small part of herself. She found it difficult to understand why she was letting herself stay in this situation. But then she came to the realization that the constant repetition of acts of abuse are not unlike the dripping of acid on porous matter. There takes place a gradual and systematic process of erosion. There comes a point of no return. Stella barely recognized herself. She had become a shell. Her face pale and her eyes dead to the world.

Finally, what followed was to give her the jolt that she had long needed.
Jack chose, in a meeting with the whole team, and in front of an important client, to verbally attack her. After he had finished, he turned to look at her. She stood quite still. Her face pale and her eyes glittering with unshed tears.
There are things that one can hide, behind closed doors, so as not to display one's shame and misery for public scrutiny and judgement. But once these things are out into the open, there is nowhere left to hide. The victim is then forced into taking some sort of action.

When Stella looked around the table, she saw that everyone seemed both shocked and embarrassed. Jack, when she glanced at him, had a look of triumph in his eyes. She had never been able to work out why he had set out to destroy her. What she had just seen, on his face, was the triumph of a torturer over his prey. She left the room. She would not be coming back here again.

Her life, over the next months, was like that of a sleepwalker. She did everything in a mechanical way, unaware of her surroundings. Emotionally, she had completely shut down. After the death of her father, Stella's mother had moved to a house on the Dorset coast. This is where she stayed, her mother taking care of her, but not intruding on her apparent grief.

Jack had tried to find her. He had tried very hard. There were letters and telephone messages. She neither opened the letters, nor did she answer the messages. After months he finally stopped.

One day, when Stella was out walking on the beach, she had a strange sensation. It was that of the first flutter of hope. For a long time, she had lived in a darkened room, in a world of nights. As she opened the curtains of this room, she could see that although the room was still dark, and outside it was still night, there was enough light to make out the outlines of her life.

Stella would recount all this to Adam when he returned. He deserved an explanation. He would better understand why she sometimes seemed withdrawn and unreachable. She would also rent out her flat. She no longer needed the security of somewhere to hide in.

When she did tell Adam about renting the flat, it did occur to him that she was not actually selling it. It still left her an important option open. But he did not mind. It was a first step. He was very sure of her.

Stella never did find the time to tell Adam about her life with Jack. She did not realize that soon there would be no point.

4

Adam's assignments abroad were becoming more and more frequent. Stella did not mind this. It was his job. She had adjusted. She would often play back the conversations that they had had together. Thinking about the times that they would be walking somewhere, and they would be laughing so hard that Stella would have to fold herself into his side and cling on to his arm, would make her smile even months after the event. She never did remember, afterwards, what they had been laughing about. All that she did remember was that there was always a great deal of laughter between them. And then there was the excitement and anticipation of his return. That made up for all the absences.

During the times that he was gone, Stella tried to fit in as much work as she could. Although a great deal of her work was mapped out months, and sometimes over a year ahead, the most important part was the changing day-to-day planning. She did her best to keep on top of this---so as to be able to spend as much time with Adam as possible when he was home.

The first weekend, after Adam had left, was difficult for her. There had been so many things planned. A meal in Chinatown, followed by the cinema. Sunday lunch with friends, and then the afternoon spent on the sofa, catching up on all the programs that had been recorded. It was not that she felt lonely, it was just that she had been so looking forward to this time together. These long weekends, where neither of them had to do any work, were becoming more and more rare.

Having made up her mind to rent out her flat, Stella decided to go there and make out a list of the things that needed to be done. The flat was not large, and any work that had to be carried out would not take much time.

She knew that Adam would be pleased with her decision. He never referred to it, but she was sure that he looked on her keeping the flat as a sort of 'get out clause'. He would have been happier, she was sure, if she had decided to sell
it. But Stella was not yet ready for that step. She had been through too much not to keep open the option of an escape route. The memory of her time with Jack was still too raw.

Both Saturday and Sunday were spent packing up clothes, the few valuable objects that she had and the rest of her books. Over the next couple of weeks, she would have everything cleaned and a local letting agent contacted. It was never to get that far.

Adam called her several times over the weekend. Although their conversations were brief, Stella was always left with a deep feeling of warmth. Not unlike an arm around the shoulder. These were memories that she would cherish in the years to come. Clinging on to them, as one would onto a liferaft in a stormy sea.

Then, once again, it was Monday morning. Her day. But with Adam being away, there was no real start or finish to the day. There was no shopping to be done, no evening meal to prepare and no flowers to be arranged. Stella would do all that just before his return. She showered and dressed. She would leave as soon as Mrs. Hughes, the cleaning lady, arrived. She had already left her a list of instructions.

Going into her study to check her diary, Stella was once again drawn to the notice board on the wall. Her hand automatically went to the invitation card for Edward Falconer's exhibition, in a fortnight's time. And once again she had the same strange feeling that she had had before. It was as if a chill shadow had passed before her. This time the shadow seemed darker, and the chill that much colder. This feeling did not leave her all day----casting a cloud over everything that she did.

She walked slowly around the flat, stopping occasionally, touching familiar objects. This was something she did when she was disquieted. It gave her a sense of the present, rather than that of what had been. Today this did not work.

Stella had a children's charity event on Thursday. She was organizing this in conjunction with two other children's charities. She had checked all the details for the guest list and the caterers. There were to be clowns and jugglers, and three bands from two different London schools. It had been in the planning for almost a year. There had been nothing left to chance. She would check everything again this evening.

Looking at the clock, she saw that it was eight-thirty. She decided not to wait for Mrs. Hughes. She needed to get out and clear her head. She would go to the nearby coffee shop to have breakfast.

Before leaving, Stella went into Adam's office. She made a note of the things that had to be done in here, adding it to the list that she had already left in the kitchen. She stood for a moment and looked at the wooden box that she had given him the previous week. She ran her hand over the mother of pearl elephant on the lid. She sat down at the desk and, after a few minutes, reached over and opened it up. There, in the top section, was the freesia bud that she had placed in the box, when she had first given him this gift. Although completely dried out and parchment like, it still held on to faint hues of blues and purple. Beside the flower, there was a small pile of pieces of paper, all neatly folded. Stella hesitated before reaching out to open one of the folded pieces. She had always respected Adam's privacy, as he did hers. She found that she could not help herself. The note, when opened, was in her own handwriting. As were all the others. They were hurriedly scribbled words--- letting him know what time they were meeting that evening, or what had to be collected on the way home. They were the pointers and the map references of their past year together. She replaced all the notes, as she had found them, gently closing the lid. These were the memories that she would later cherish.

Leaving the flat, Stella found herself smiling to herself, as she walked to the café. This was a side of Adam that she had not expected. Her mood had lifted. The earlier feelings of foreboding were receding. This was not to last for long. The following days were about to become a game of shadows.

Reaching the café, she found a table by the window, and having ordered a coffee, she took a newspaper from the rack beside her. Turning to the Arts page Stella found herself staring at a picture of Jack. He was holding up some sort of an award. There was a tightening in the pit of her stomach. A return of clearly remembered fears. She looked at the picture more intently.

Seemingly seeing him for the first time. The eyes that she had, sometime ago, thought were hiding depth and intensity, were only masking a coldness and a controlled rage. The mouth that she had run her finger along, and tasted so deeply, was nothing more than a line of cruelty and anger. She felt herself trembling as the memories started to erode all the partitions that she placed between herself and the past.

Stella thought back to her time with Jack. The memories were coming back in a rush now. Hammering at the door of her consciousness. Uninvited guests, demanding to be let in. The unexplained absences, the dinners prepared and left to get cold, the violence of a lovemaking that left her body bruised and her mind dulled. Yet she had accepted it all. His constant and unceasing verbal attacks had left her too exhausted to make any decisions. Acceptance was her only easy option. That was until that last day. The meeting at the film studios.

The memory of that day would always be etched on Stella's mind. Jack had come home early, the evening before. She had been quite astonished. The meeting the next day was with a potential new client, and she had assumed that he would be working late at the office. He had poured them both a glass of wine, taking the drinks out into the garden. After they had sat down, he started to speak. His voice was less confident than usual, his manner unusually subdued. He spoke about the importance of the next day's meeting. The funding that it would provide for the future. He spoke of their life together. How happy it had made him. Listening to him, Stella could not reconcile the two sides to this man. The night before, he had come home some time after midnight. She had prepared dinner for nine o'clock. He had neither spoken to her, nor offered her an explanation. This morning, he had left before she had woken. He had leant forward then, gently touching her face, reading her thoughts.

'Things will be different from now on,' he said. 'I promise.'

Stella smiled but said nothing. Even the smallest gesture of kindness from Jack was enough to make her forget the loneliness of her nights, the disillusion of her days. And, as always, she had felt grateful. That night he had held her until she had fallen asleep. When she awoke, the next morning, he had already left.

Jack had left her a note by the coffee pot, saying that he would see her at the office, and that he would book a table at the Italian restaurant, near his house, for that evening. It was the first time, in a very long while, that she felt there was to be some hope for their future together.

Stella dressed with great care that morning. A simple black linen dress and low-heeled shoes. The dress had been a present from Jack. He would approve. Lately she had found that, more and more, she needed his approval.

When she arrived at the film studios, she felt both confident and well prepared for the meeting. Little did she realize that this day would bring the ending of a chapter, both in her personal and professional life.

The meeting started well. There was a great deal of excitement and enthusiasm, from all the team, over the proposed project. Three low budget films, to be made back-to-back, with the funding for all three in place.

Then it was Stella's time to speak. She spoke about the projected timelines and the projected budgets. She then turned her attention to her ideas on the promotion of these films. The early press releases, the ones that would be ongoing throughout and the intensive promotional campaigns, these to be carried out at the completion of each film. It was then that she became aware of a strange tapping sound. Not unlike that of the slow hand clapping that one hears at football matches, when the fans are trying to demoralize the rival team. She looked around and saw that it was Jack. He was hitting the table with the palm of his right hand. His face was quite impassive, but his eyes told a different story. Stella was suddenly very afraid of what was coming.

'Your work is mundane, 'Jack said. 'It's pedestrian. Your ideas are dull. There's not a shred of originality. You would be more suited to doing promotional campaigns for afternoon cookery shows. I take the full blame for this. Even after all the time and guidance that I invested in you, I failed to see that you could neither understand, nor translate our ideas.'

Stella thought that he had finished, but he had not.

'And the way you are dressed. It's more suited to a gathering of suburban housewives, in a suburban wine bar. This is a film studio, Stella. It's a bloody film studio,' he said, bringing his fist down hard on to the table.

There was a measured silence in the room. She sat looking down at her clenched hands. When she finally looked up, the faces around the table told

The Unreal Dance

their own story. There was compassion and pity. But no-one was shocked. This was just Jack being Jack. He was one of their own. She was not.

Stella left without a word, only bowing her head slightly towards the others.

She went back to his house, packing quickly, making sure that there was no trace of her life here left behind. A last look at the bedroom did not provide her with any answers that she might be looking for. There was no sense of any tenderness. She had been sharing a bed with a stranger.

The confines of the bedroom can be a treacherous place. Secret and shadowed. Lies told, promises made, illusions fragmented beyond repair. The balance of power between two people changed. The mind not wanting to accept any truths.

Sex is a harsh and clinical word. Each letter seemingly forged from hardened steel. Each letter with sharp edges. If placed on a pair of scales, with the word love, it would carry the heavier weight. Love is a gentle, rounded word, with a soft, often blurred outline, its weight being measured only by its endurance.

Stella shook herself. One glance at a photograph in a newspaper, and an intruder had forced itself into her mind.

Leaving the café, she decided to take the side street that she always took and make her way to the park. She would first stop at the shop that sold the antique bottles that her mother used to collect. She had seen a dark green decanter in the window that she had liked, the last time that she was passing. Over the years the shop's owner, Maurice Albrecht, and her mother, had formed an unlikely friendship. When they went to his shop, he would offer them tea and small, delicate, ginger and cinnamon biscuits that his wife had baked. He would recount stories of his earlier years in Poland. Each time a different one. Sometimes Stella asked him to repeat one that he had already told, and he would laugh, saying that his life was not unlike a book of short stories, and she could always go back to the one that she had liked. These were such happy memories. They helped edge out those with Jack.

Reaching the shop, she found that it was closed. She had never known Mr. Albrecht to close on a weekday. There was no note on the door. She would pass by again on her way back home.

Next, Stella went to a shop that specialized in antiquarian maps, atlases and globes. She had seen a nineteenth century map of the world, the last time that she was here. It was highly detailed, and the various countries were beautifully coloured in. She would buy it for Adam's birthday. It would hang in his study. The shop owner said that he would keep it for her until she was ready to collect it.

When she reached the park, Stella immediately made her way to the pond where she had seen the two children, the week before. She remembered their small faces, so intent on guiding their sailboat. But they were not there. The school holidays were over. She had had a strange longing to see them. Almost imagining that they belonged to her and Adam.

She suddenly realized that she had had nothing to eat since last night. She made her way to her usual Turkish restaurant. As always, it was quiet on a Monday. She ordered her food and a glass of wine. When the food came, she just picked at it. She had little appetite today.

Stepping out into the street, Stella felt a wave of loneliness wash over her. It was as if there was a glass partition between her and the outside world. She stood still for a few moments, deciding what to do with the rest of the day. There was no food to get, no flowers to be collected, no conversation to look forward to tonight. She deeply missed Adam. She took the telephone from her bag and made a call. The call was answered on the second ring.

'Patricia. Can you come over tonight?'
'Is there something wrong, Stella?'
'No, not really. Adam's away and I can already feel the evening stretching out in front of me.'
'I'll be there around seven o'clock.'

Stella's mood lightened. She and Patricia had been close at school and had grown closer over the years. She was the keeper of Stella's secrets. And Stella, hers. It was an unconditional friendship. Something they both nurtured and respected. She had read somewhere that one's miseries should always be delivered into safe hands. Stella's had been.

Her day suddenly had a purpose and a framework. She would go to the Greek delicatessen to get food for tonight. She would then make her way home, stopping at Mr. Albrecht's glass shop, to see if he still had the dark green decanter that she had seen in his window last week.

When Stella got to the glass shop, it was still closed. She was to learn, the following week, that he had died. She was deeply saddened. Another full-stop on a sentence. Another chapter closed. We seem to go through our days with the assumption that the landmarks of our lives will remain unchanged. But we have to live with dull pain that this is never so.

When she arrived home, there was a message from Adam on the answering machine. He would not be able to get back in time for her charity event, but that he would definitely be home by the weekend. He said that he missed her beyond measure. Stella smiled at that.

She unpacked the food, in the kitchen, laying everything out on a large platter, ready for the evening. She poured herself a glass of wine and put on some music. Country and Western. Each song a complete short story. Loves lost, marriages shattered, lives troubled.

She had always likened the love affair, between two people, to a series of dances. The cha- cha- cha would be the initial dance. Two people meet. There is a spark. The dance reflects the flirtatiousness and the possibilities between them. The Bosanova takes them to the next stage. The stage of exploration. The stage where they know that there is something there that must be pursued. This is the time of discovery. Then there is the Tango. A dance of tension, passion and jealousy. All the things that inevitably come with love. Then there is the Ghost Dance. When love has gone, when you are dancing alone, with your arms around someone who is not there.

Patricia arrived a little after seven o'clock, a bottle of chilled champagne in one hand, and a bag containing cheese and black grapes, in the other. She could sense that Stella was troubled, but she did not comment on this. Stella would only talk when she was ready. She remembered that it was some months after she had started to live with Jack, that she had voiced her doubts about her relationship with him. And that was after Patricia had noticed the bruising on her wrists and forearms.

'It's not what you think,' Stella had said at the time, 'Jack's lovemaking can get a little rough sometimes.'

The subject was never brought up again.

The evening went well. Stella started to relax. She then told Patricia about the photograph of Jack, in the newspaper, how it had affected her, the memories persistent and invasive.

'He's gone, Stella,' she said,' he's long gone.'

Stella nodded, but did not seem to be convinced. There are those that need not be present in a room, for them to be there. The mind is a vast space that houses many ghosts.

After Patricia had left, she went and sat, for a while, at Adam's desk. She ran her hand over the wooden box, reminding herself of the life that she had now. But her sleep, that night, was not easy.

5

Stella spent the next few days finalizing the preparations for the fund-raising party. She worked with the other charities involved, making sure that they had plans for anything that might go wrong at the final hour.

In the event very little had to be adjusted. The children had seemed transported by the entertainment, and the donations had been more than generous. She moved from group to group, thanking each for their support. She then made her way to the bar. It was here, while she was waiting for her drink to be served, that she sensed someone, standing close beside her. A familiar presence. Stella slowly turned her head. She found herself facing Jack. But it was not the Jack that she remembered. His eyes, once so intense, were now dull. His mouth, once so articulate, now had a meanness about it. She had no fear of this man standing before her. He had lost his power over her. She picked up her drink and walked away, before he could say anything.

That night Stella's sleep was deep and dreamless. And the morning brought a sense of peace that had long eluded her. Her thoughts on Adam's return, that night, she set about planning her day. She would work until after lunch, then shop for food, the fridge now being almost empty.

While she was making coffee, Patricia telephoned. She noticed a well-remembered lightness, in Stella's voice. She seemed to have emerged from behind the shadows. The ones that she had been retreating to, for a very long time. When Stella told her about the encounter with Jack, she understood. Jack had finally lost any hold over her. A ghost laid. A door closed.

It was late afternoon, by the time that Stella had time to sit down. The fridge stocked, the flowers arranged, her thoughts on Adam. She kept glancing at the clock, overwhelmed by anticipation.

When Adam did get home, a few hours later, he found her fast asleep on the sofa. Her legs drawn up toward her chin, both hands placed neatly, under her right cheek. Although he did not want to wake her, he felt too impatient to wait. He shook her gently, so as not to startle her, and folding her into him, he pressed his lips to her forehead. He held her like this for some moments, until she was fully awake. He then helped her to her feet and, cupping his hands around her face, he looked at her intently, seemingly re-memorizing each feature on her face. She looked, somehow, different to before he had left. He knew that she always looked forward to seeing him. Even if he had only gone to the office, for the day. But there had been a sense of reserve, previously. There was no reserve now. There was an openness about her manner. Something had changed. He smiled, kissed her again on the forehead, going to the kitchen, to get them both a glass of wine.

'Did you get that list of ingredients I emailed you, Stella?' he asked.

'Yes, Adam. Even down to the clams that you wanted. The ones from a small fishing village outside of Naples. Collected by a fisherman called Antonio, whose wife Elizabetta has borne him four sons and three daughters….'

'That's enough, Stella,' he laughed. 'All I did was ask you a simple question.'

It had become something of a pattern. When Adam came back from a trip abroad, he would cook the dinner. While he prepared and cooked the food, Stella would sit near him, a glass of wine in hand, asking him about the work that he had done, and telling him about hers. This had become their time together, after being apart. They tried neither to make, or answer,

any telephone calls. The area of the kitchen would become their own private world, for a few hours. There is always a gap that needs to be bridged, an awkwardness that needs to be overcome, between the departure of the traveller, and his return.

She now sat watching him. Adam's preparations were methodical. His absorption in his work complete. All the ingredients for the dish that he was preparing, in separate bowls, lined up in front of him. The garlic chopped, the flat-leafed parsley, waiting to be cut up at the end, the clams in a colander, under running water, in the sink. When Stella cooked, there was chaos in the kitchen. This had always surprised Adam, as in all the other areas of her life, she was, almost obsessively, organized and tidy.

When the food was almost ready, Stella got up and lit the candles. The table had already been set, the wine opened.

They lingered at the table long after they had finished eating. Neither had even bothered to clear the dishes away---they were so deep in conversation. They were not just talking; they were seemingly drinking in each other's words.

Adam reached out his hand and covered hers.
'Have you made any plans for the weekend?' he asked.
'No. I thought I'd wait until you got back. See how much work you had to do, see what the weather was like, see what mood you were in, see if Mars was aligned with Venus. Why do you ask?'
'My parents would like to meet you,' he laughed. 'They suggested Sunday lunchtime.'
They had lived together for almost a year now. He had always gone to see his parents on his own, never suggesting that she join him.
'I'd love to,' she said. Stella had long wanted to meet them. To put him in a different context to the one she knew him in. She had also noticed, from what he had said, that the invitation had come from them. Perhaps they had realized that there was something permanent, within the relationship between her-self and Adam. It appeared that, even in her absence, she had been accepted. She prayed that they would not be, in any way, disappointed.

That night, their lovemaking was both intense and gentle. Adam had, in the past, felt a hesitation, a reserve, on Stella's part. Again, he realized that something had changed. In the time that he had been away, she had seemed to have found a sense of peace, emerging from a dark and private place, that she had never spoken of.

When Stella awoke the next morning, she could hear Adam preparing the breakfast. She took in all the scents and the sounds. She had slept well, all her ghosts having left her alone, for once. She felt safe. Adam had managed to mend what Jack had broken.

Adam spent most of Saturday morning working in his office, attending to the mail and the various messages. He would occasionally stop for a cup of coffee, finding Stella to discuss the rest of the day's plans.

Stella was going around the flat attending to the tasks that she normally did. Loading the washing machine, unloading the dishwasher, collecting items to be taken to the dry cleaners. These were the tasks that she did every week, without even thinking about them. Today they seemed different. It was as if she was performing these acts for the very first time. She felt that she was re-living the moment that she had moved in to live with Adam. There was a hope and an excitement about the day. Her fear of Jack had evaporated, taking with it the shadow that had been her constant companion, these past few months. She went into Adam's office, standing behind him for a moment, then put her arms around him, kissing him on the back of his neck.

Adam said nothing. Just briefly squeezing her hand, before getting back to his work. When Stella had left the room, he put down the papers he was working on and sat staring out of the window. Something had definitely changed. He smiled to himself. She was not normally this demonstrative, this playful. But he knew better than to question her. She fiercely guarded her privacy, only revealing things when she was ready to.

A few moments later, Stella re-appeared.
'I'll give you exactly half an hour to finish whatever it is that you're working on. I have a craving for Chinese food, that is stopping me thinking about anything else. So be kind.'

Adam got up and pulled her to him.
'I'm ready now. You have no idea how much I've missed you.'
'Me too,' she said. 'Me too.'

The day, though a little chilly, was clear and bright. They walked for most of the way to the restaurant in Chinatown, Stella's hand tucked into Adam's elbow, his hand covering hers. They talked little, both absorbed in their own thoughts.

When they reached the restaurant, they could see, through the windows, that it was crowded. Adam opened the door for Stella and gave her a gentle push into the room.

'You go first,' he said. 'You're sure to get a decent table. I think the manager likes the colour of your eyes.'
'Absolute nonsense,' she laughed. "But it might have something to do with the size of the tip I leave, each time.'

When the manager saw them, he smiled and guided them over to a table that would seat four people. They were regulars here. They always ordered too many dishes. A table for two would not be large enough.

When their order had been taken, they just sat and smiled at each other for a few moments.

'A whole weekend,' he said. 'A whole weekend together, Stella. I honestly can't remember the last time.'
'Not quite a whole weekend together. We'll be with your parents tomorrow. And that's making me nervous.'
'There's no need to feel nervous. There's absolutely no need. Anyway,' he smiled, 'it's about time that you all met.'
There was a seriousness, in Adam's voice, when he said this. As if he had made up his mind about something. This was not lost on Stella.

When they left the restaurant, the brightness of the day had gone. A sharp wind had come up and it had started to rain. Adam suggested that they should take a taxi home. Every time that he used the word 'home', she felt a gentle warmth spread throughout her. It was as if she could feel an arm around her shoulder, a safety that she could count on.

The rest of the day was spent watching some of the programmes that Stella had recorded, in his absence. They would occasionally stop to talk or have a drink. She felt a sense of comfort and contentment, that she would remember, long after. That night, their lovemaking had a depth and a passion that was new to them both. Adam held close, until she fell asleep.

When she awoke next morning, she could hear Adam, in the kitchen, preparing breakfast. He was humming tunelessly, to himself, as he laid out the plates. She slipped on a dressing gown and joined him. He noticed that she looked a little nervous.

'You have a right to look nervous,' he said. 'My parents are truly terrible people. Really frightening. My mother will first make you clean the house and then set about cooking the lunch. So, you must do your best, darling.'

'And what will the three of you be doing,' she laughed, 'while I'm doing all this?'

'We'll be nursing the gin bottle. And discussing the weather.'

The drive took a little over two hours. Adam's parents had moved to a small village, outside Brighton, some years ago, when they had both retired. They had both wanted to be near the sea, but also near a city, so that they would not miss the life that they had had, in London.

On the way, Adam stopped at a small nursery that specialized in roses. After carefully looking around, he chose a standard rose, already in bloom, and covered in a mass of buds. The flowers were of a pink, so pale that they were almost white. Their scent heady, in the warmth of the day.

'My mother is a passionate gardener,' he said. 'But you'll see that, when we get there.'

The approach to the house was through a driveway, with a wall of eucalyptus trees on either side. The house, itself, sat proud and square, in the middle of a large, brick-walled garden. Stella had the impression of entering the pages of a fairy-tale. Adam's parents, hearing the sound of the car, were walking toward them.

'Mr. and Mrs. Cavanaugh,' Stella said, holding out her hand.

Adam's mother laughed. 'Brendon and Meg, please. Welcome, Stella. Your visit is long overdue.' With that she stepped forward and kissed Stella on both cheeks. His father, after looking at her hard, for a moment or two, smiled at her and gave her the warmest of hugs.

"We've been looking forward to seeing you for a very long time,' he said.

Adam looked on, with some amusement. His parents had been asking to meet Stella, almost from the first moment that he had talked of her. Perhaps sensing the importance of her place in his life. He went back to the car and collected the rose bush that he had brought for his mother, and the bottle of single malt whiskey that he had brought for his father.

They went into the house, through a panelled hallway, leading to the sitting-room, where a drinks tray had been laid out.

Adam watched Stella closely. No longer nervous, she moved with ease, noting all the objects, absorbing all the details. She was not unlike a cat, entering a new territory, choosing a place that it would settle. He could not believe that he had only known her for a year. It seemed to him that she had always been part of his life.

'I've booked a table at our local pub for lunch,' Brendon said, addressing Stella. 'It's always difficult meeting someone for the first time, knowing what their likes, and dislikes, are. And I thought that we'd come back here, for coffee, afterwards. Meg has been dying to show you the gardens.'

The pub was delightful. A long bar area, with two small dining rooms, at either end of it. The scent of the burning logs mingling with that of the food.

The conversation over lunch was relaxed and light-hearted. But underneath all that, Stella was aware that Adam's parents were trying to get to know her, as she was them. Meg asked her about the work that she did. She seemed both knowledgeable and interested in Stella's ideas on charities. The two men talked about cricket, and the dismal performances of the England team, so far.

It was quite late when they returned to the house. Lunch having taken longer than any of them had anticipated. After they had had their coffee, Meg showed Stella around the gardens, naming the plants and telling her when each would be in full bloom. She then collected large handfuls of herbs, from the separate herb garden, for Stella to take back to London, with her.

'Adam tells me that you have a love of cooking,' Meg said. 'I'll put these in a sealed bag, before you leave. They will keep for quite a long time in a cool place. The rose that you brought, my dear,' she continued, 'is called 'Gentle Hermione'. Not unlike you, Stella. I'll plant it outside the conservatory door.'

With that, they both went back into the house.

The day had gone well. Both Stella and Adam were reluctant to leave. But the drive home was a long one, Adam having to prepare for an early morning management meeting, the following day.

'Please come back soon,' Meg said. 'Come back very soon.'

It was to be a long, long while before Stella saw Adam's parents again. The fabric of her life having been torn, and shredded beyond repair, by that time.

6

Monday morning. Stella awoke a little after seven o'clock. Adam had already left. She had heard him moving around earlier but had gone back to sleep. She lay on her back, for a few minutes, planning her day ahead. She decided that she would call Patricia, to see if she would be free for lunch. She felt that she would like some company today. She rarely saw anyone on a Monday, enjoying the freedom of having no plans, of not having to be anywhere at a given time. But Patricia was different. Her presence never intruded on Stella.

She went into the kitchen. While she was making the coffee, she sat down to make a list of all that she would need to do today. She thought of the bag of fresh herbs that Adam's mother had picked for her. She would make a simple herb and lemon roast chicken, served with a chicory and mint salad, followed by cheese and fruit. Stella poured herself a cup of coffee and, opening the fridge, she took out the bag of herbs. The different herbs, each tied individually with string, brought back the memories of yesterday. Memories she would always cherish. They had treated her with a warmth that had made her feel as if she were a part of them. Not a guest, but someone dear that they had not seen for some time. They had made enough of a fuss of her, to make her feel special. But not so much that she would feel, in any way, awkward. She was grateful for that.

At eight-thirty Stella telephoned Patricia. She knew that she would find her at her desk, at the magazine offices, where she worked.

'Can you meet me for lunch, Patricia?', she asked.
'Is there something wrong, Stella? You so rarely share your Mondays with anyone.'

'No. Nothing wrong at all. I'd just like your company. I thought that we'd go to the Polish restaurant near here.'

'I'd like that. I'll call you when I'm out of my meeting, and on my way.'

Stella went into her office. She had to check her diary for the work that had to be done and make a list of the telephone calls that had to be made. As she reached for her diary, she noticed two, beautifully wrapped, parcels on her desk. One she recognized, from its size, as the perfume that she always wore. She picked up the second package. It was long, in shape, wrapped in matt black paper, bound together with a dark purple ribbon. She looked at it for a moment, then unwrapped it carefully. It was a leather box. Inside, along the silk lining, was a heavily woven bracelet, in rose gold. Beside it she found a card. It read 'With all my love, Adam'. Stella gazed at it for a long time, then put it on her wrist. It was quite exquisite. She picked up the telephone and called his private line, at the office. Adam was not at his desk. She left a message on his voice mail. 'Thank you', she said. 'Thank you.'

Patricia was already at the restaurant when Stella arrived. They ordered without even looking at the menu. Potato pancakes and smoked salmon. A bottle of red wine. They sat talking long after they had finished eating, comfortable in each other's presence. It was after three o'clock when they left.

Stella bought the food for dinner and collected her usual order of flowers. The afternoon was turning cold. She went back to the flat. Here there was a message from Adam, saying that he would be home around six o'clock. She smiled. She had not expected him until much later.

The days that followed had a pattern. Adam would come home in the evenings, working while Stella prepared dinner. They would sit at the kitchen table talking, long after they had finished eating. Often, they would walk to a nearby bar, to have coffee. Sometimes she felt that they went out, because they so much enjoyed coming back. There was, for both of them, an excitement about these routines, that had not yet paled.

The weekend brought storms. The rain heavy, the winds strong. They ordered take-away food and watched old films. They laughed about all the long weekends they had planned but never taken. They sat with road maps and destinations, planning yet another one. Adam reminded her about Edward's exhibition, the following Thursday. Stella told him that she had underlined in red, in her diary. They were both sorry that the weekend was almost over.

Thursday arrived. The day of Edward's exhibition opening. Stella felt nervous. When meeting a man's parents, and when meeting a man's closest friend, there is an unconscious seeking of their approval. There is an unwritten test to be passed. She was sure that his parents had taken to her, as she had them.

But what of Edward? He and Adam had grown up together. They had shared each-other's secrets. What would he make of her? It was inevitable that he would compare her to the previous women in Adam's life. Would she be found wanting? She hoped not.

Adam had arranged to meet her at the gallery. He said that she would find him somewhere near the entrance.

When Stella arrived, she saw that the gallery was already crowded. There was a large poster, on both of the glass panels, on either side of the entrance, announcing the exhibition. 'Echoes From the Wilderness'---The sculptures and paintings of Edward Falconer.

She was just reaching into her handbag to take out her invitation, when she saw Adam coming toward her. He took her by the shoulders and brushed his lips against hers.

'Let's get a drink, and then I'll show you around.' There was a great deal of pride in his voice. 'Even though I'm familiar with Edward's work,' he continued, 'I'm always surprised by the scale and magnificence of it all. I'd like you to see the exhibition before I introduce you to him.'

He took Stella's hand and guided her towards the rooms housing the sculptures. The first room held two of the larger works. They were of a man and a woman. They were separate yet looked as if they belonged together. They looked at, yet past each-other. As if they were bound by grief and loneliness, rather than love. Stella felt profoundly disquieted.

The next room held the smaller sculptures. These too were lonely figures. Outsiders.

But it was the third room that captured Stella's attention. The sculptures were of children. Graceful, rounded bodies, caught in the time between hope and experience. Small, plump hands, holding on to larger ones. Being guided, being shepherded. It brought to mind the story that Adam had told her, about Edward, and the younger sister, who had been found drowned. She stood looking at it for a long time. Trying to imagine what had come before, and what had come after.

Adam took her hand and led her through to the rooms housing the paintings.

These were haunting. Again, lonely figures, against lonely backgrounds. Caught in the moment between a dream, and an awakening. The eyes sightless. The shadows parting, not to reveal the light, but the dark void of an abyss.

'Let's go and find Edward,' Adam said. 'It's time that you two met.'

It was the moment that would change Stella's life. And Adam's.

Edward saw them and came over. Adam introduced them.
'Stella, Edward. Edward, Stella.'
'I'm glad that you could both come,' Edward said.
He shook Adam's hand. Then he took Stella's hand in his, turning it palm upward, looking at it, as if he was trying to read it. He did not ask them what they had thought about his work. He looked into Stella's eyes. He knew that she had seen what he could see. Pain is something that one easily recognizes in others.

'Shall we all meet for dinner next week?', Edward asked.

'I'm afraid that I'll be travelling a great deal, for the next few months. I will be back, but only for a couple of days, at a time. I'll get Stella to call you. She'll know when I'm back in London. Come to dinner.'

'I'll look forward to it.' With that he abruptly let go of Stella's hand and walked away. She looked down at her hand, as if she was seeing it for the first time. As if it no longer belonged to her.

Over dinner, Adam apologized.
'I'm sorry, Stella. I didn't know, until this afternoon, that I would be going away again so soon, and for so long. The investigation that I was covering, into the irregularities, at the bank in Hong Kong, seems to have spread much farther. A second whistleblower has come forward. There appears to be not only the breaking of the sanction laws, but also the handling of drugs money, and that of arm's dealing. It is, in effect, a network of sophisticated money laundering.'

'It's all right, Adam. Of course, I miss you when you're away. But I was more than well aware of what your work entailed, from the very beginning. We still have a few days. We can sit and plan that long week end you're always promising me.'

'I always keep my promises, Stella,' he laughed. 'I always keep my promises.'

Adam asked her what she had thought of Edward's work.

'I found it all rather disturbing. It was as if the figures, in all his work, were carrying with them the heavy weight of their past, toward a future, with no hope. And the sculptures of the children were of those who, unknowingly, had been poisoned at their roots. The most haunting, though, was the painting of a young man, holding the hand of a child, a small dog following them, its head bowed down. You could feel the depth of the despair. When I looked more closely, I saw that the eyes of the young man were blank, as if he did not want to see what lay ahead.'

'That painting,' he said, 'is Edward's story. 'The tragic death of his young sister, Lily. Something he never talks about, something he will never get over. There is, in life, a point when a heart is so badly broken, that it can never be mended. You are forever doomed to carry around the fragmented pieces with you. The memory of the pain your constant companion.'

Stella said nothing. She was thinking about the look in Edward's eyes. So intense, so remote. He had withdrawn to that place, in the mind, that afforded him some shelter. Waiting to be reached, waiting to be saved.

That night, and the nights that followed, Stella had deeply troubled dreams. Of children reaching out to her, crying tears of blood. Of gnarled, old hands, on young plump wrists. Of vast, empty wastelands, with no boundaries. She would often cry out in her sleep. Adam would wake her, holding her until she found some calm. She would lie still in his arms, afraid to go back to sleep.

7

This time when Adam left, Stella felt a great sense of loss. Afraid that the safety-net that he had so carefully woven for her, might start to unravel. She wandered around the flat, constantly looking at the telephone, waiting for his usual call from the airport. When it came, she felt an overwhelming sense of relief. She had somehow thought that maybe he had forgotten.

'I'll be back in a week's time. It'll only be for a couple days, I'm afraid. I'm already missing you,' he said. 'Take great care of yourself, Stella.'

'And you too, Adam.'

Stella looked at her watch. It was almost twelve o'clock. She would go out and buy the Sunday papers, then stop somewhere for lunch. Until she had started to live with Adam, she had hated Sundays. For her, it was a day with little purpose. A day with no start, and no finish to it. She felt apart from the outside world. It was a day of couples, holding hands and talking to each other. It was a day of families, chattering, or quarrelling amongst themselves. All going somewhere. But, with Adam, all that had changed. She had become part of that outside world.

When she returned home, Stella saw that there were two messages on the answering machine. One was from a woman called Helen, asking Stella if she would be able to have lunch with her, sometime this week, to discuss the new project that they would be working on. The other was from Patricia. She knew that Adam had left, and could she come around to see Stella. She had something to tell her. Stella smiled to herself. She could easily guess what this was. She first called Patricia, to let her know that she could come around anytime that she wanted. She then called Helen, saying that any day towards the end of the week would be fine.

Patricia arrived less than half an hour later, carrying a bottle of chilled champagne. Stella smiled. She knew what was coming next.

'I've met a new man,' she said, uncorking the bottle.
Stella went to fetch two glasses.

'I know that this time it will work out. He's different.'
'They've all been 'different',' Stella laughed, going on to list all their names.
'That's extremely ungenerous of you, Stella. I may have made a few mistakes in my time. I'm the first to admit that.'
By this time, Stella was helpless with laughter, wiping away her tears, with the back of her hand.

The afternoon passed, with the two of them, seemingly reverting back to their teenage years.

Evening had set in. Patricia had left. Stella, suddenly very much alone, afraid of the dreams that the night would bring.
Monday morning. Stella had awoken early. It had not yet been light. Her dreams had, again, been vivid and troubling. She decided that she would not spend the day on her own. She did not want to be alone with her thoughts.

She sat down at her desk and started going through her diary. I was not yet six o'clock. It would be a long day.

At nine o'clock, Stella started on the list of telephone calls that had to be made. The new project that she was involved in was the largest and the most complicated that she was to work on, to date. There were four charitable organizations that would be working together. Three children's charities, and one for the homeless, setting up workshops and work training centres. There was to be a gala dinner, in the autumn, for five hundred guests. The main event, of the evening, was to be an auction, with two professional auctioneers.
There had already been offers from art galleries, antiquarian book dealers and jewellers. The security would have to be tight.

Stella worked late into the afternoon, stopping occasionally, for a cup of coffee. She went out for a walk, to clear head. It was only when she returned that she realized how hungry she was. She had not eaten all day. She laid out some cheese on a plate, warmed up some olive bread and poured a glass of red wine. After she had eaten, she tried to watch a film on the television but found that she could not concentrate on it. She took a sleeping pill and went to bed early. This pattern, of her evenings, continued until Adam returned the following week.

The week went by quickly, Stella putting in long hours, and taking early nights. She was missing Adam far more than she usually did.

When Adam came home after the weekend, the first thing he noticed was how tired Stella was looking. She had lost weight and had shadows under her eyes. But he did not remark on this. If there were anything worrying her, she would tell him, in her own time. He hated being away from her so much, but he had little choice.

The next two days passed quickly. They would both start work early, Adam going to the office, and Stella working from home. They would meet at lunch time, spending the rest of the day together. This time, Adam would be gone much longer. He did not expect to return for at least three weeks. But he did say that he would be home for at least a week. He told Stella to book them into a hotel, somewhere remote and isolated. She had laughed at that but said that she would do it.

Adam hated leaving her this time. Three weeks suddenly seemed far too long. He had been away for much longer periods in his working life. But he had had no-one to come back to before.

Before he had left, Stella had held onto him tightly, not wanting to let go. Her thoughts on all the empty nights, stretching out in front of her.

After Adam had left, Stella, once again, settled into the routine that she had established before. That of long working days, and early nights. She was aware that she was deliberately tiring herself out, so that her nights would be dreamless. They were not.

Coming home late, one evening, after a meeting that had gone on too long, she found Edward on the doorstep, leaning against the railings, smoking a cigarette. Stella showed no surprise. It was as if she had been waiting for this. Not knowing when it would happen but knowing that it would.

'Shall we go and get something to eat?' Edward asked.
Stella nodded. She had lost the power of choice.

They had been walking for about fifteen minutes, in complete silence, when Edward stopped outside a small Italian restaurant. He opened the door, letting her go in first.

They were shown to a corner table. Stella looked down and saw that there was a card with Edward's name on it, resting against the candlestick. He had reserved the table.

'Would you like red or white wine, Stella?' He asked, with some amusement. He had noticed her looking at the card.

Stella was startled. These were the first words he had spoken, since she had found him on her doorstep.
'Red please,' she replied.

Edward ordered the wine. Again, the silence, while they chose their food. The waiter returned with the wine, pouring a little into each glass, and took their order. Edward raised his glass in a silent toast. Stella did the same.

'Tell me a little about yourself, Stella. But only a little. This is going to be a long journey. And I want to find the way myself.'

Throughout the meal, Edward would ask her the occasional question, about herself. He listened attentively to her replies. He did not once talk about himself, nor did he ask her what she had thought of his work. There were long silences, where she would find him looking at her, but not saying anything. This was not a man to find comfort or safety with, she thought. This was a man who would emotionally disembowel you, leaving you with little.

The walk home was wordless, as before. Edward waited until Stella had unlocked the front door. He said his goodnight, abruptly turning and walking away.

When Stella went to bed that night, she realized that it was the first time, in a long while, that she had not thought of Adam.

The next morning, while she was making the coffee, Stella noticed that there was a message on the answering machine. It was from Adam. He said that he would try and call her the next day.

Stella's day was spent going from meeting to meeting. Each charity putting forward their own ideas on how the fundraising event should be approached.

When she got home, she saw that Edward was again there. Waiting, exactly as he had been the evening before. Standing on the doorstep, leaning against the railings, smoking a cigarette. There were two brown paper carrier bags, at his feet.

'May I come in, Stella?' He asked.
'Yes,' she said, unlocking the front door, and leading the way to the first floor flat. There was a given acceptance, on her part, that she had not questioned.

Edward handed Stella the smaller of the two carrier bags. He had put together a picnic supper. The bottle of red wine that was in the carrier bag, was the same Tuscan wine that they had drunk last night. He had noticed that she had enjoyed it.

They ate at the kitchen table, neither of them saying much. This was not the companionable domesticity that she shared with Adam. There was a tension, an intimacy, that made Stella both nervous and uncomfortable.

When they had finished eating, Edward went to the hallway and brought in the second paper carrier bag that he had had with him. He took out a small sculpture. It was that of two hands. The small hand of a child, held firmly in that of a larger one. It was beautiful.

'I noticed you looking at it at the exhibition. Going back to it, again and again.'

Edward did not wait for her to say anything. He picked up his coat, said goodnight, and left.

It was to be several days before Stella heard from him again.

Adam called later that night. She was glad to hear his voice, hoping that he would still the confusion that was taking hold of her. She missed him. She needed him here, to help protect her from herself. She felt herself being drawn into an unknown territory, from which there would be no return.

After Adam's call, Stella sat for a long time, looking at Edward's sculpture. Without the rest of the body, the two hands were suspended in isolation. Like the central part of a story. You could write both the beginning of the story, and the ending of the story. Here she found some hope.

When she went to bed that night, it was to a night of deep, untroubled sleep. Having talked to Adam, she had reclaimed a sense of calm and reason.

All this was to be gone a few days later. Stella was roused from her sleep, by the sound of the sound of the telephone ringing. She looked at the bedside clock. It was just after five.

'It's Edward, Stella. I'm sorry to wake you up so early. I've been working all night. I needed to speak to you before I go to bed for a few hours. I'll pick you up at seven, this evening.' And with that he put the telephone down.

Stella was astonished. He had not even asked if she would be free that evening. When she tried to call him back, all she got was the engaged tone. It was the same all morning. He had taken the telephone off the hook.

Her anger did not last long. When she went into her study, the first thing that she saw was the sculpture on her desk. She realized then that this was a man that dealt in a different currency, to others. He expected to be understood by his work, not himself. He had called her at five o'clock in the morning, not out of disregard, but to convey that it was important that he see her.

Edward arrived at seven o'clock. The first thing he did was to hold up his hand, in a gesture of apology.
'I'm sorry I woke you so early, Stella. I'd been working for over thirty-six hours. It was important that I see you. Get your coat, I've got a taxi waiting downstairs.' He went down ahead of her.

When Stella reached the street, she saw Edward standing by the taxi, holding the door open for her.

'Where are we going, Edward?' She asked.
'To my house.'

The rest of the journey passed in silence. A silence Stella was becoming accustomed to. No longer uncomfortable.

The Unreal Dance

Edward's house was two houses, converted into one. The original facades having been kept.

Unlocking the door, he showed her in. Stella sensed an impatience in him.

'Follow me,' he said, moving toward the staircase.

When Stella reached the top, he was there, waiting for her.

Edward showed her into the space that was his studio. A space spanning both houses. Skylights, with blinds, going from one end, to the other.

He tugged on her arm, with some impatience, as one would with a child that were lagging behind. He guided her to the far end of the room, placing her in front of a wall, covered in sketches, some small, and some almost life size.

'Tell me what you see, Stella,' he said. 'Tell me what you really see.' He turned away, leaving the room.

Stella stood there for a long time. Seeing, at first, the same figures that she had seen in the paintings, at the exhibition. The same men. The same women. The same children. The same bleak landscapes. Then, looking again, she started to see a slight difference. Imperceptible, at first. The figures did not look so lonely. Not so doomed to accept whatever the Gods were handing down to them. The landscapes had the start of an outline, faint, but perceptible. So now the story, being told, had a starting point. These figures looked as if they might have hope. They might have a choice.

Stella turned away from the sketches. Edward was standing there, looking at her intently, an expression of triumph in his eyes. He had been right, the first time that he had met her. She really was able to see what he could see. He took her hand, the way one might that of a child, leading her downstairs.

'Come. Sit down. I'll get us both a drink. I certainly could use one,' he said.

It suddenly dawned on Stella, looking at him, that Edward too, had changed. The intensity, the impatience, they were both still there. But there was also a new gentleness. This was something that had not been there before.

Edward handed Stella a glass of wine. He poured himself a large whiskey. He did not sit, instead pacing up and down, occasionally glancing at Stella. As if, having come to a decision, he walked over to where Stella was sitting. He pulled her to her feet, his eyes not leaving her face.

'I saw the way you looked at my work, upstairs,' he said. 'I saw that you understood. For me, you've brought back the memory of a happier place. A place that I'd thought long gone.'

Stella was silent. She had seen a torment, in his eyes, that was no longer there.

'Take me back to that place, Stella. Be with me.' Edward gently traced the outline of her face, with his hand, as though he were trying to memorize it.

Stella showed no surprise at his words. There had been an inevitability about all this, from when first they met.

Edward smiled. He had recognized her acceptance. He took her coat, gently draping it around her shoulders, making no move to touch her. Physical contact would cloud her judgement. He dropped her off at her front door.

Stella no longer knew who she was. She had lost herself. In all this, neither she, nor Edward, had given thought to Adam.

And so, the dance began.

ACT II
LIES AND BETRAYAL

Betrayal can lead us down the darkest of paths. Into the darkest of rooms, of a Hogarthian hell. To the edge of the abyss, that houses the worst of our demons.

8

Stella stood on the outside steps, and watched Edward walk away. He did not turn around. After a few moments, she opened the front door, taking the stairs to the flat.

When she let herself in, she felt a sense of disquiet. She looked around, as if she was seeing this place for the first time.

The familiar had become unfamiliar. As if the furniture, and all the objects, had been re-arranged. But she realized that, in the space of one evening, it was her life that had been re-arranged.

Stella sat down on the sofa; her coat still draped around her shoulders. She felt as if she had walked into someone else's life. An intruder, into her own past.

The telephone rang several times, but she did not answer it. Instead, she sat, holding her secret. This secret did not, as yet, have shape or form. Its presence only being felt by its weight.

It was late, but she had no desire to sleep. She walked around the flat, stopping for a few moments in each room, trying desperately to make some sense of her thoughts. Finally, she settled in her study. Sitting at the desk, she reached out to touch the sculpture that Edward had given her. The two hands, firmly holding on to each other. The one, leading the other.

When Stella awoke the next morning, it was from a troubled sleep. Dreams of row upon row of people, walking past her, staring sightlessly into the distance, unaware of her presence. She had called out, but her voice was left unheard.

She made a pot of coffee and sat at the kitchen table. It was Sunday. She had no plans. She would take a long walk and perhaps stop somewhere for lunch. She thought about calling Patricia but decided that she would rather be alone. She knew that she would not hear from Edward. Although left unsaid, she realized that he would wait to hear from her, when she was ready.

Thoughts of Adam crowded into Stella's head. Thoughts of this past year. All her happiness being replaced by confusion and uncertainty. Adam had taken her, a damaged and fractured person, and made her strong. The shadows in her life had faded and become contained. The realization that she was about to shatter what had been built, brought about a depth of despair that she had not felt for a long, long time.

She dressed quickly. She needed to get out, to leave these surroundings. The burden of the decisions that she had to make, weighing heavily upon her. As she reached the front door, the telephone rang. She knew it would be Adam. She would have to take it.

'Stella? Where have you been? I've been worried. I called until quite late last night.'

'I'm sorry,' she said. 'I was out having dinner with Patricia and was too tired to check for messages when I got back.'

And so, the lies started. The sure and certain path to betrayal.

'I'll be back at the end of the week,' he said. 'I'm taking some time off, so you can start getting out all those road maps, and hotel brochures that you've been saving. I'll call you before I leave. I miss you more than I can say.'

If Stella hesitated, Adam did not notice. 'Me too, Adam. Me too,' she said.

Stella left the warmth of the flat, walking out into a damp and grey day. Again, she was wearing one of Adam's sweaters, but this time the scent of him provided her with no comfort. Only a reminder of what was to unfold. A story that filled her with both fear, and excitement. An unknown territory, with no memories or substance.

She walked across the park, not stopping to look at the children by the pond. She walked through streets, unaware of those around her. It had started to rain. Light at first but getting heavier with each step. She seemed not to notice. The light was fading, and a bitter wind had come up. When Stella looked at her watch, she saw that it was after five o'clock. She had been walking for almost six hours. She had not stopped for lunch. She had felt no hunger. She suddenly realized that she was shivering. Her hair, and her clothes, wet with the rain. She would take a taxi home.

When she reached the flat, she had trouble opening the door. Twice the keys fell from her hand. The cold had reached right into her; the shivering having taken a complete hold.

Even the warmth of the flat did not seem to get through to her. Stella knew that she should get out of her wet clothes, but she was too exhausted. She fetched a small rug, wrapping it around her shoulders. She made her way to the kitchen and poured herself a large brandy and sat by the radiator. After a while, she went into the sitting room and lay down on the sofa. She fell into a fitful sleep. It was here that Mrs. Hughes, the cleaning lady, found her, the next morning.

When Mrs. Hughes came in, she realized that there was something wrong. The door to the flat was not closed, and all the lights were on. Stella was huddled up on the sofa, her face flushed, and her breathing laboured. She went over to her and gently shook her. Stella's eyes slowly opened but showed no sign of recognition.

There was a list of telephone numbers, kept on a pad in the kitchen, in the event of any emergencies. Mrs. Hughes called Patricia's number. She would know what to do.

Patricia arrived about an hour later. Together, they managed to get Stella out of her still damp clothes, and into the bed. Her fever had got hold, and the shivering had got worse. She was oblivious to both Mrs. Hughes and to Patricia, seemingly not knowing where she was. She cried out occasionally, but the words were unintelligible. Patricia called Stella's doctor, Howard Feingold. He arrived shortly after.

After examining her, Dr. Feingold asked the two women how long Stella had been like this. Mrs. Hughes said that she had seen her the previous Monday, and Patricia said that she had talked to her on the Friday, and she had seemed fine then.

'Is Adam away?' he asked. They both said yes.
'She can't be left on her own. I'll give her some medication, but it might be a while before it starts to take effect.'

Patricia said that she would take time off from her work and stay with Stella. Mrs. Hughes said that she would come in, each morning, to tidy and do any shopping that was needed.

He wrote out a prescription, and asked to be called, should Stella get any worse.

The next two days proved to be difficult ones. Stella not seeming to respond. She refused food and would only accept small amounts of sweet tea. On the third day, Patricia called Dr. Feingold. He could hear the anxiety in her voice and said that he would come around that afternoon.

Howard Feingold had been Stella's doctor for some years. And until the episode with Jack, he had rarely had occasion to see her. It was then that he had seen the bruises on her body and had been made aware of the bruises on her psyche. The bruising on her body had faded. But those on her emotions had taken a great deal longer to heal. This time, when he examined her, he felt a familiar sense of disquiet. Physically, she was improving. The fever had lessened; the infection was responding to the medication. But there was a look of pleading in her eyes. She seemed not to want to get better, clinging on to her illness as a protection, against something that she could not face. As if it provided her with a temporary refuge. But now was not the time to probe. He would have to wait until she was stronger.

After he had left, Patricia looked in on Stella and saw that she had fallen asleep. She went into the kitchen and poured herself a glass of wine. She took this into the sitting room, where she would be able to hear Stella, if she called out. There was something puzzling her. Twice, last night, Stella had called out Edward's name. And once she had grasped Patricia's wrist, pleading with her to fetch Edward. Not once had she asked for Adam. Stella had seemed distracted over the past weeks, avoiding meeting her. A story was slowly dawning on Patricia. A story that filled her with dismay. She hoped that she was mistaken.

Adam arrived back two days later. He had telephoned to say that he was returning, but his call had gone unanswered. As he climbed the stairs to the flat, he felt an overwhelming longing to be with Stella. He was smiling to himself as he unlocked the front door, thinking of the days ahead. This was to be the first time, in a long time, that they would be spending a length of time together.

Patricia, hearing Adam's key in the lock, went to greet him. She had picked up the message about his time of arrival, only this morning.

If Adam was surprised by her presence, he did not show it. She took his arm and, wordlessly, guided him to the kitchen. Here she poured them both a drink and indicated that they should sit down.

'Where's Stella?' he asked. 'Is she still at work?'

Patricia explained, as calmly as she could, that Stella had been extremely ill, but that she was recovering well. Her work team had been contacted, and all her meetings had been covered. She would need a period of rest. She was still very weak. Mrs. Hughes had come in every morning. And Patricia had come in after lunch, sitting with Stella, and staying the night.

Adam, looking worried, went in to see Stella. She was asleep. Her face pale and drawn, dark shadows under her eyes. The illness had taken its toll.

When he went back into the kitchen, he saw that Patricia had laid out a light supper. A platter of cheeses, a salad, and warmed bread. He was grateful for her company. It was a shock, to him, to see Stella like that. He had never seen her look so vulnerable. So lost in another world.

They ate in near silence. One, occasionally, asking the other a question. After the dishes had been cleared, Patricia showed Adam the various medications that she had laid out on the side, with a note of the times that each should be given. She told him that the doctor had been, three times, and that he would be coming again the following afternoon. And that if Adam needed to go to his office, she would come and sit with Stella. She left shortly after, having first looked in on Stella. She hoped, fervently, that Stella would not call out Edward's name during the night.

After Patricia had left, Adam looked in again on Stella. She was still asleep. He went into his study to deal with his mail, and to see to any messages. But he was unable to concentrate. Stella had obviously been extremely ill. He felt that he should have been there for her. To have been the one to look after her. The depth of what he felt for her both overwhelmed him and surprised him. He was, by nature, reserved. He sat, for a while, staring into nothingness, thoughts crowding into his head. He went back into the bedroom.

The Unreal Dance

Stella was still asleep, her breathing uneven. He sat down on the bed, taking her hand in his. She was murmuring something. But he could not catch what it was. He went and fetched a cold cloth, laying it gently on her brow. She slowly opened her eyes, but did not seem to recognize him. It was fanciful on his part, but he thought that she looked almost disappointed, as if expecting someone else.

That night he stayed on the sofa. He would be able to hear her if she should call out. Once, during the night, she got up to go to the bathroom. He went to her, but she did not seem to see him. She moved as a sleepwalker.

The morning did not bring much change. Adam sat her up, gently, giving Stella her medication. She opened her eyes, but again seemed not to know who he was, or where she was. He went into the kitchen to make her tea. He felt quite helpless.

When Mrs. Hughes arrived, she was surprised to find Adam there. She had not known that he would be home. She asked after Stella.

'I honestly don't know how she is, Mrs. Hughes. I've given her pills, but she has hardly touched the tea that I made. She seems to have little strength,' he said. 'I want to thank you for all the help that you've given. I can't help wishing that I'd been here. I would have returned earlier, if I'd known.'

Mrs. Hughes assured him that his being here would not have made any difference, as Stella had been in a state of unconsciousness for most of the time. She then suggested that Adam change Stella's night clothes, while she made the bed. After this she would make some more tea, and perhaps, between them, they could get her to eat something.

Adam was glad to have something to do. He had little difficulty in changing Stella's nightgown, only stopping to notice how painfully thin she had become. How very frail.

The day passed slowly. Adam went out to buy flowers, the ones that Stella liked, while Mrs. Hughes cleaned the flat.

When he returned, he saw that Mrs. Hughes was smiling. Stella was sitting up, she said, and had managed something to eat. He put the flowers down and went straight away to the bedroom. Stella was sitting up, against a mound of pillows. She smiled at him weakly, reaching out to him. He took both of her hands, in his.

'You've had us all so worried,' he said.
'Ah. The lengths I go to, to get attention,' she laughed.
'Perhaps, next time, you could find a less dramatic way?'
'I'm sorry, Adam. I went for a long walk on Sunday. The heavy rain was sudden. I had trouble finding a taxi. When I got home, I was too exhausted to change my clothes and must have just fallen asleep on the sofa. I realize that it was stupid of me.'

Adam looked at her, for a long time. Then he reached over, and brushed a strand of her hair, away from her face. He had been frightened when he first saw her, last night. He had thought, then, that if, ever, anything were to happen to her, he would not be able to face the loss. He could not imagine his life without her.

'Would you like more tea?' he asked.
Stella said she would.

The flowers had been arranged. Mrs. Hughes was just leaving.

'Thank you, again,' Adam said. 'You've been very kind.'

A short while later, Dr. Feingold arrived.

'I'm glad that you're back, Adam. I've been very worried about Stella. I'm certain that your being here will help a great deal. I'll just go and examine her, if I may.' With that he went into the bedroom, closing the door behind him. He wanted to talk to her. He felt that that would be better in private.

'Dr. Feingold,' Stella said. 'How kind of you to come. I'm feeling much better today.'
'Good. You've had a rather bad chest infection. Your temperature was dangerously high. If it were not for the fact that your cleaning lady found you, so soon afterward, you'd be in hospital now.' He took Stella's temperature and examined her chest. Her breathing was much better.

He sat back and looked at her.
'Is there something troubling you?' he asked.

'No,' she said, avoiding his gaze. 'I'm just a little anxious about all the work that I should have been attending to. Nothing else.'

Dr. Feingold looked at her intently. He wondered whether he should go on. He decided he would.

'When I first came to see you,' he said, 'you were quite delirious. You kept calling out a name. 'Edward', I think. You were insistent that I should find him.'

'The only 'Edward' I know,' she said, 'is a friend of Adam's. I have only met him the once. At the opening of his exhibition. I think that you must be mistaken.'

Howard Feingold said nothing. As well as being a doctor of medicine, he also had a reputation of being a formidable psychologist. The human mind, and the human behaviour, held little mystery for him. There was always a pattern. To reach the truth, you had to piece together that pattern. He knew that Stella was hiding something from him. He had known her a long time. She would go to him, when she was ready.

After Dr. Feingold had left, Adam went in to sit with Stella. He could not get over how fragile she looked. She smiled at him, but her eyes were bleak. She seemed to have taken refuge, in a world of her own. A world that did not allow him in. Again, he had that sense of helplessness.

'Would you like to get up?' he asked. 'I can make you quite comfortable, on the sofa.'
'Thank you, no. I'm feeling rather tired. I'd like to go back to sleep.'
Adam rearranged the pillows and kissed her on the forehead.
'Call me if you need anything,' he said. 'I'll be in my study.

Stella did not want to sleep. She wanted to be alone with her thoughts. They tumbled, one against the other, like clothes, in the drum of a tumble-dryer. She wanted to see Edward. He would help her make sense of all this. He had a strength, a strength that she did not possess. Tears coursed down her cheeks. Tears, not for herself, but for Adam. Tears, for the inevitability, of what was to unfold.

9

As the days passed, Stella grew stronger. And so, too, did her misery. Adam had turned down an assignment, not wanting to leave her, until she was completely recovered. This left her with a weight of guilt, her now constant companion.

A routine established itself. Every morning, Adam would help Stella bathe and get dressed. After lunch, he would leave for his office. Patricia would come around, in the late afternoon, staying until Adam returned. The few hours that Stella had to herself, were spent looking sightlessly, into a seeming void. A void that offered no answers, nor any comfort.

One evening, when Adam came home, he said that he had run into Edward, earlier that day. Edward had looked startled. At first, not appearing to recognize Adam. It was as if he had seen a ghost.

'He looked wretched,' Adam said. 'He seemed quite lost. And his eyes had that shuttered look, that look that they had had some years ago, when his sister died. He asked me how long I had been back. I told him that I'd been back about three weeks. How you'd been extremely ill, and that I didn't want to go away until you'd fully recovered. I said that I'd be working at the office, every afternoon, and would he like to meet for a drink, one evening. He didn't reply. He just turned and walked away.'

Stella had a hunger for more details about Edward. It was more than a hunger. It was a greed. But she said nothing.

The next day, after Adam had left, Stella went into her study. She had to make a start on her work. There was a great deal of catching up to do. There was a long list of telephone calls, to be made, and a pile of reports, on all the

The Unreal Dance

meetings she had missed, to be gone through. As she was reaching for the telephone, the doorbell rang. It was Edward.

They stood looking at each other, for some moments. Not moving. Not touching.

'I gather you've been very ill,' he said.

There was no sympathy in his voice, no compassion. The words were delivered as a harsh accusation. As if he had been cheated out of a part of her life. Stella understood.

Edward paced around the room, not saying anything. When he finally turned to look at her, his eyes were bleak.

'I waited for you to call me,' he said. 'I gave you time. There was a promise, Stella. There was a promise.'

'I know,' she said, quietly. 'And the promise will be kept.'

Edward walked over to her and gently touched her face.
'Have you talked to Adam, yet?' he asked.

'How could I? For weeks now, I've been slipping in and out of a sleep. And when I was awake, the thought of what we're about to do, what has to be done, has drained all strength from me. We've betrayed him, Edward. We've betrayed him.'

'I'm not a fool, Stella. Adam has been the only true friend I've ever had. And I'm taking away the one precious thing in his life. I am aware of the depth of the hurt, and the damage that will follow. But we have no choice, you and I. There was no choice, from when first we met.'

'Give me time, Edward. Give me a little more time.'

He looked at her with an intensity that she found disturbing.

'Come to me when you're ready, Stella.' With that, he left.

When Edward left, Stella was overwhelmed with a loneliness that seemed to wrap itself around her. These walls no longer offered her the comfort that they had, in the past. Everything seemed temporary. There was no real substance. She realized that she would have to tell all this to Adam. But she was not yet ready.

Adam came home, a little after seven o'clock. He was carrying a large package.

'This is for you, my darling,' he said, dropping a kiss on her head. 'Go on. Open it.'

Stella had difficulty opening the box. Adam helped her. Inside was a long, dark green, waxed, riding coat. It had a wool lining, and a hood. Both could be detached. It was quite beautiful. She felt the start of tears.

'In case you decided to go walking in bad weather, again,' he laughed.

Stella looked at the coat, then put it down. She went over to Adam, and putting her arms around him, rested her head on his chest. Her heart was starting to break.

'Do you feel strong enough to go out to dinner?' he asked.
'I'd love to,' she said. Stella was glad to get out. In truth, she felt that she no longer belonged here.

The next morning, Adam left for the office quite early. Stella was fully recovered, and no longer needed either care, or help. Before leaving, he told her that he had made her a pot of coffee, and that he would be back at the usual time. And that if she needed anything, she was to call and let him know.

Stella's heart sank. They were back to their established routine. The one she had so cherished, over the past year. The one that had given her the stability, and comfort, that she had searched for, all her life. She was faced with the realisation that there would be little chance of any of that, with Edward. She knew that her life with him would be one of constant uncertainty. She would have to change, and adapt, to his structures, to his frameworks. There would be little peace between them.

After she had showered, Stella stood, for a long time, in front of the bathroom mirror. She carefully examined her face, looking for any changes. She was certain that the burden, of her lies and betrayal, would have somehow left some mark. But there was nothing. But then, she thought back to Jack. Until, toward the end, she had not noticed any changes in him, either. It was much later that she learned about the other women in his life. She had believed all his excuses about working late, at the studios. All his excuses, for missing the dinners, she had so carefully prepared.

After she had dressed, Stella sat down and made a list of the shopping that she had to do. It was Adam's birthday on Saturday. She would go first to the shop, where she had bought the map for him, and arrange to have it delivered the following day. She would then shop for the food for dinner and collect the flowers that she had ordered. She had, already, reserved a table, at the Greek restaurant, for the night of his birthday. On the Sunday, they were going down to have lunch with his parents. The thought of the last, filled her with great sorrow. She gathered, to her, the memories of that other Sunday. The warmth, and the kindness, that Adam's parents had shown her. The way that they had, so unconditionally, accepted her, into their lives. Each day seemed to bring, with it, more tears, in the fabric of her life.

Over dinner, that evening, Adam told her that he would be going away the following week. It would be for two weeks. Stella felt a sense of great relief. She had bought time.

'You'll be alright, won't you?' he asked.

'What? With two weeks of not having to do any cooking, cleaning, or feeding the goats? I think I'll manage to get through it,' she joked.

Adam reached over, covering her hand, with his.
'You have no idea how much I miss you, each time.'
Stella said nothing. There was little she could say.

On Saturday, the day of Adam's birthday, Stella got up early. She prepared a breakfast of lightly scrambled eggs, warmed rolls and wildflower honey, and a dish of ripe, scented peaches and apricots. She set the table, placing a small vase of pale, cream roses, at the centre. She collected the framed map, and a card, from her study. She sat and waited for Adam to come out of the bathroom.

When Adam finally came into the kitchen, he was genuinely surprised.
'Stella? What's all this?'
Stella got up from the table, going over to kiss him.
'Happy Birthday, Adam.' She handed him his present.

The look on his face, when he opened the framed map, would stay with her, always. It was of such delight, and gratitude.

'My God, Stella, this is absolutely amazing. Where, on earth, did you find this?' Putting the map down, he put his arms around her, resting his chin on her head, not wanting to let her go. She gently moved out of his arms, to attend to the breakfast. The realisation came to her that this would be the last birthday that she would be spending with him. She was filled with a deep, deep sadness.

After breakfast, Stella asked him what he would like to do that day. 'This is your day, Adam, we'll do whatever you want.'

He looked at her for a while, smiling then.
'The usual?' he asked.

When Adam was home, their Saturdays had a pattern. They would take the side streets toward the park, stopping at the bookshops, and the small antique shops, on the way. They would then decide where they would have lunch and would make their way there. Today, when Adam asked her where she would like to have lunch, she laughed.

'I don't mind', she said. 'But it will have to be something light. 'Tonight, I'm taking you out to a lavish and elaborate feast. Dark secluded corner, candles on the table, and mournful music, in the background.'

Adam stopped and turned her toward him.
'You spoil me, Stella. You really spoil me. I cannot even begin to imagine what my world would be like, without you in it. You've woven such magic into it. Thank you.'

Stella, again close to tears, marvelled that he was still so unaware of the changes in her. She had taken to deception well.

Later, that night, when they returned from the restaurant, Adam asked her if she would join him in a drink. She could see that he was reluctant to let the day end. But she had been taken over by an exhaustion that had taken hold of her. Her mind weighted by confusion and turmoil, her limbs seemingly unwilling to support her body. She said that she was tired, barely able to keep her eyes open. He looked disappointed, but he understood. It had been a long day. He went over to her, placing his hands on her shoulders.

'Thank you for today, Stella. Thank you for everything.'

Stella watched him, as he poured himself a drink, and walked toward his study.

'You go to bed, darling,' he said. 'I'll join you in a little while.'

When Adam finally came to bed, Stella feigned sleep. She could feel him, standing beside the bed, looking down at her. She could, almost, reach out and touch his happiness.

Next morning they left early, to avoid the Sunday traffic. To Stella, the journey seemed longer than she remembered. When they reached the house, Megan and Brendon were already outside, ready to greet them. They had been waiting for the sound of the car, coming up to the driveway.

Megan went over to Stella, held her close, for a moment, then kissed her on both cheeks. She noticed how pale Stella looked, how painfully thin. Adam had told her that she had been ill, but that she was recovering well. But there was something else. There was a reserve about Stella, that had not been there, when last they met. Brendon, stepping forward to hug Stella, also became aware of this.

When they went into the warmth of the house, the scent of the wood polish, mingling with the scent of the flowers, made Stella dizzy. She held onto the sideboard, pretending to examine a Chinese vase that was standing there. Adam had noticed and went over to her.

'Are you all right?' he asked. 'Do you want to sit down?'
'I'm fine,' she said. 'It was just coming into the warmth.'
Adam looked concerned. He would keep an eye on her.

The lunch went well, with Adam and his father, deep in conversation, about the cricket. And Megan asking Stella about her work.

'Brendon, and I, would love to come to your next charity function,' she said. 'Adam is always telling us how much work goes into them, and how well they always turn out.'

'The next one is in the autumn,' Stella told her. 'I'll let you have the details, nearer the time.'

Megan noticed that Stella was looking at her, with a strangely wistful look in her eyes. The last time that Stella, and Adam, had been here, they had constantly glanced at each other, as if they had been sharing a secret. This time it seemed that Stella was holding on to a secret of her own. She felt disquiet for her son.

After lunch, as with last time, Megan showed Stella around the garden. She took her to a flowerbed, where all the flowers were various shades of blue, against a background of silvery grey eucalyptus. The violet verbena, covered in butterflies, the paler blue scented stocks, and the last of the dark purple, elegant irises. It was like an intricately woven shawl that someone had let fall, and left, forgotten. Although a warm day, Stella felt herself shiver.

They next went to the herb garden. Here, Megan picked handfuls of the different herbs, tying each bunch with string. These were for Stella. She remembered how much she had enjoyed them, last time. They made their way back to the house, Megan pointing out the various plants, on the way. She noted Stella's silence, her perceptible withdrawal.

When they returned to the house, Adam could see how tired Stella was and suggested that they should leave.

As she was about to get into the car, Megan came up to her. She put her hand on Stella's arm, giving it a gentle squeeze.

'Take great care of yourself, Stella. And my son.' She watched them, as they drove away.

The days, before Adam went away, were difficult for Stella. Her nights were troubled, her days more so. Adam's leaving filled her with both immense sadness, and immense relief. But it was only to postpone what was to come. In the days after Adam had left, Stella immersed herself in her work. She worked from early morning, until late at night, only stopping to eat. She was not unaware that she had, yet again, found another way of not dealing with what had to be dealt with. But that time had now come. She picked up the telephone and called Edward. He did not answer. She left him a message, saying that she would like to see him. He called back, almost immediately.

'Stella?'
'I'd like to see you, Edward.'

'Shall I come and pick you up?' he asked.
'No. I'll come to you.'

When Stella arrived, Edward was already at the door, waiting for her. He turned her to face him, looking at her for a long time, as if he was drinking her in. He took her hand, and led her up the staircase, to the bedroom. The room was large, and high ceilinged. The long windows, facing the bed, giving an impression of a wall of glass. Edward crossed the room and pulled down all the blinds. Although not in complete darkness, there was little light. He then went over to where Stella was standing.

'Close your eyes, Stella,' he said. 'Keep them closed. I don't want you to see me with your eyes. I want you to learn me, as I will you. I want you to learn the texture of my skin, I want you to learn the scent of my body.'

He undressed her and laid her on the bed. He then undressed himself and lay down beside her. His hand traced the outline of her face, moving down, slowly, to the curve of her lower back. Stella reached out to touch him. Her touch, at first tentative, became more sure. Edward could feel her impatience but stilled her. There was time. When he finally made love to her, it was with a gentleness, and a tenderness. There was no urgency in his lovemaking. That would come later.

Afterward, they lay beside each other. Not speaking, not touching. There was no need for either. A pact had been sealed. A promise had been kept.

When they went downstairs, the light had started to fade. Edward turned on a lamp and went into the kitchen. He came back with a bottle of wine, and two glasses. The wine was chill, and fragrant.

Stella looked over at Edward, answering his unasked question.
'I'll tell Adam, when he gets back.'
The thought of this, pained them both.

It was still early, when Stella returned to the flat. She felt a sense of the calm that had eluded her for so long. Now she had no doubt, she had no fear. She picked up the telephone and called Patricia. They had not spoken in some days. This was unusual for both of them. Stella needed to talk to her. To explain why she had remained so silent. Until now, she had not been ready.

'Stella?' Patricia said. 'How are you? I've been worried about you.'

'I need to talk to you, Patricia. It's important. When will you be free?'

Patricia, hearing the urgency in Stella's voice, decided that she would have to leave the piece that she was working on, for the magazine, and go to meet her.

'Have you eaten yet, Stella?' she asked her.

'No. No, I haven't. Would you like to eat here, or shall we go out?'

'I'll come around. We can then decide.'

When Patricia arrived, Stella suggested that they go out to eat. She needed to talk to Patricia about Edward, but felt a great sense of disloyalty, sitting at Adam's table. In Adam's flat. She was slowly disengaging herself from these surroundings. She was as someone, passing through.

'There's a small Italian restaurant that I've recently discovered. Shall we go there? It's only a short walk away.'

'That sounds good,' Patricia said. She noticed that Stella, though still looking rather pale, and tired, after her illness, seemed to have gathered a new strength about her. A new resolve.

Stella tucked her hand into the crook of Patricia's elbow, and led her to the restaurant, where she had first eaten with Edward. Here, she knew, she would feel his presence. The manager, having worked in the business of restaurants, for some years, was able to recognize those who had come, just to eat. And those who had come to talk, needing a place of privacy. He showed the two women to a quiet corner table, a little way away from the other diners.

Patricia waited, until after they had ordered, and the food had been brought, to question Stella.

'Stella?'

'I'm leaving Adam,' she said. She noticed that Patricia showed little reaction.

'You don't seem surprised,' Stella said. 'I had, somehow, expected you to be shocked.'

'I am shocked,' Patricia said. 'But not surprised. When you were feverish, you kept asking for someone, called Edward. You never, once, asked for Adam. I can only assume that you're leaving Adam, for this 'Edward'. I don't know the man. I've, not once, heard you speak of him. This is, in itself, rather unusual. That you're contemplating such a step, without even speaking of it, to me.'

Stella was looking down at her hands, on the table. She finally looked up, meeting Patricia's gaze.

'I've wanted to talk to you about it so many times. I did try. But my mind was in such a state of confusion. Of uncertainty. Each day that passed, I became more, and more aware, of the enormity of what I was about to do. My thoughts were incoherent. My emotions, so unsteady.'

'So, who is Edward, Stella?'
'Edward Falconer. The man whose exhibition Adam, and I went to.'

Now, Patricia did look surprised.
'Are you talking about Adam's friend? Adam's best friend?

Stella nodded, again, staring down at the table.

'But you've only known him a few months. When, on earth, did all this start?'

'I think, in all truth, it started that night. That night, when I first met Edward,' she said. 'I wasn't looking for anything, Patricia. I honestly wasn't. You've known me long enough to know the truth of that. I was so happy with Adam. I wrapped myself, in the generosity, of his love. And, with each passing day, the shadows of my past receded. Do you think that I wanted any of this?' Stella had barely touched her food. She sounded wretched.
'It happened, Patricia. It just happened. There was no choice, for either Edward, or myself. There is no choice. No other way.'

They both sat, for some moments, in silence. Patricia spoke first, reaching out her hand, to gently touch that of Stella's.

'You know that I will always support you, in anything that you do. But have you, really, thought this through? It will, almost certainly, have such devastating consequences. The damage that all this will do to Adam, will be long lasting. The hurt, and the pain, deep. Be careful, Stella. Be very careful. You may, never again, be able to have what you have now. The step that you're taking, is going to define your future years.'

'I know,' Stella said, quietly. 'I have thought of nothing else.'

The days, before Adam's return, settled into a pattern. Stella arose early, working until the afternoon. She would then go to Edward. There was to be little conversation between them. They would come together, wordlessly. Even afterward, not speaking much. Neither wanted to hide behind words. Without words, the mind was stripped bare. Stella never offered to stay the night. And Edward, never asked. He knew that deception did not come easily to her. It was not in her temperament. He had seen her torment, of the past months. She could not live in two places, at the one time. Her life, with Adam, would have to end. Before hers, with him, could begin.

Stella was aware that Edward's impatience was growing stronger, with each passing day. Waiting for Adam's return. She would, often, catch him looking at her. With an expression of such uncertainty. Afraid that she might change her mind. She would, then, smile at him, gently. To let him know that she understood. That, she was sure. That, for her, there would be no turning back.

Two days before Adam's return, Stella went to Edward, as had become usual. But this time, as she followed him up the staircase, he did not stop at the bedroom. Instead, he took her hand, and led her to a room, on the floor above. The room was quite beautiful. Large, and spare. There were four glass doors, leading onto a balcony that ran the full length of them. In the centre of the room, sat a long desk, and a hard-back chair. On one wall, there was a small painting. Stella went over, to look at the painting. Edward stood silently, watching her.

The painting was that of two figures. As were almost all of Edward's paintings. But immediately, Stella was aware that this one, differed greatly, from those she had seen before. The figures were that of a man and a woman. The man, holding the woman's hand, looked down at her, with the warmth of love. She looked up at him, with a look of complete trust. This painting portrayed hope. It portrayed a beginning. Stella, leaning forward, saw that there was a line of writing beneath the two figures. The line read, "There is no more you and I, only us". A line she recognized, from Omar Khayam. When she turned to him, she saw that Edward was watching her, intently.

'I thought that you'd like this room, as your study. I'll build you bookshelves and get you anything else that you might want. I want you to be happy here, Stella.'

'I will be happy here, Edward. I already am.'

It was strange to see Edward, so unsure. His vulnerability, so rarely glimpsed, brought out a protectiveness in Stella. This was something that she was unused to. Thinking back, it was she, who had always relied on the strength of others.

When Stella left, she did not go straight home. As she had reached the gate, leading out of Edward's courtyard, she had looked back, toward the house. She saw Edward standing in the doorway, framed, as a figure, in one of his own paintings. It was then that she felt the true weight of the responsibility that would befall her. Her misery had developed into a solid form. Its density, not allowing any light in. She realised that she could not face the emptiness of the flat. The echoes of a past happiness that had promised so much. It was a place that she had already left. A place now neglected.

Reaching home, Stella could not remember where she had walked, or how long she had walked. All that she realised was that to some extent, the turmoil in her mind had stilled. As she unlocked the front door to the flat, the telephone was ringing. It was Adam.

'I was just phoning to remind you that I'm coming home, the day after tomorrow. Just to make sure that you're not out on the town with Patricia, have not run off with another man, or set light to our home. I miss you so much, Stella. Perhaps, we can find a way of you spending a little time with me, while I am away. If it doesn't interfere with your work. Anyway, we'll talk about that when I see you. I really can't wait, darling.'

As she put the telephone receiver down, Stella found herself choking on her tears. A part of her, wishing that she had never met Edward. But she knew this to be a lie. Edward had taken her and shaken her awake. Her past life now seemed like a dream, within a dream. A place where misery, and comfort, had danced together. Had become true companions. Each, in turn, taking the lead, in this dance.

That night, when Stella went to bed, she fell into an exhausted sleep. She dreamed that she was in a long corridor, with doors, along the length, of both sides. Although the corridor was dark, she could still see, quite clearly. She would call out to people that she knew, but they walked past, not seeing her. She knocked on all the doors, but none were opened. She looked up, seeing Edward, standing at the end of the tunnel. But as she made her way toward him, he turned and walked away. When she awoke, the pillows were wet, with her tears. Her limbs were aching, and her head was muddied, from the stagnant pool, of her dreams. It was early, not yet light. Stella was tired, but she could not face going back to sleep. Nor could she face getting up, and coming to terms, with the day.

10

Stella was sitting at the kitchen table, making a list for the shopping, when the telephone rang. It was Patricia. Her voice sounded concerned.

'I remembered that Adam is coming home tomorrow,' she said. 'I don't want you to be on your own today, Stella. I've arranged to finish work after lunch. Shall I come over to you, then?'

'I'd like that,' Stella said. There was gratitude, in her voice.

It was when she had returned, to sit at the kitchen table, to continue with her list, that the futility of what she was doing came to her. Out of habit, she was making a list of all the meals she was planning for the following week. Out of habit, she was making a list of all she would need to make those meals. It suddenly came, to her, with a great sorrow, that for her, and Adam, there would be no more meals. There would be no following week.

Stella walked around the flat, occasionally stopping, to pick up a book, or to touch an object. Trying to commit these things to memory. A reminder of a time, filled with light. A light that would, soon, be put out.

Patricia arrived a little after two o'clock. She noticed that Stella looked tired and distracted. Her eyes, red from tears. An air, of an almost, tangible weight of resignation, and inevitability, shrouded around her.

'Let's go out, Stella,' she said. 'You need to get away from here. You've made your decision. Staying shut up, here, with all your thoughts, is going to drive you mad.'

Stella nodded, in agreement.

'I know,' she said. 'But it's only now that the finality of what I am doing has really hit me. I've just been buying time, making excuses. I've not given thought to the unfairness, of all this, to Adam. I should have told him about Edward, from the very beginning. I feel such shame, Patricia. Such shame.'

They walked for some time, in silence. Stella, absorbed in her own thoughts, barely noticing the outside world. Patricia, hoping that Stella had not placed herself, on a path of self-destruction.

The rain had started to come down. Light, at first, but fast becoming heavier. Patricia, mindful of Stella's recent illness, suggested they should return home. Stella looked at her blankly, seemingly not able to understand. She had retreated to a place of her own. Patricia understood. She had seen Stella like this before. It was the only way that Stella knew of protecting herself, against the shadows, cast by her thoughts.

Once home, Stella lay down on the bed, falling asleep, almost straight away, not waking until some hours later. The light had already faded. She stared into the darkness, feeling very alone.

Patricia, watching from the doorway, felt a tide of pity wash over her. For Stella. For Adam. Thinking back, to how she had envied them, their happiness.

'I was going to make us something to eat, Stella,' she said. 'But there's absolutely nothing in the fridge.'

'No. I'm sorry. I can't even remember the last time that I did any shopping.'

Patricia looked over at her. Stella, always so organized, so precise. Now looking fragile and lost.

'It really doesn't matter,' Patricia said. 'We can order food, to be delivered. I'll set the table and open a bottle of wine.'

It was late, when Patricia left. She had settled Stella, in the bed, as she would have, a child. She would wait to hear from her.

When Stella awoke, the next morning, it was still dark. After she had showered, she, again, looked into the bathroom mirror. She, again, looked for any changes, in her features, that she might have missed. There were none. Her face, instead, was a mask that jealously guarded, all the lies, all the deceptions. And her surroundings, although also remaining unchanged, were no longer a home to her. They were just a place, a place where she used to live.

Stella dressed quickly, shaking herself out of a lethargy that had taken hold of her. She would go to the shops. There was no food in the fridge, no fruit in the fruit bowls, no fresh flowers, in the vases. She could not let Adam come home to this. He was due to return in the late afternoon.

Laden with bags, and flowers, Stella returned to the flat, two hours later. The cupboards were stocked, the fruit bowls were filled, the flowers put into water. As she went through these motions, she felt that, somehow, she was setting the scene for a tragedy, waiting to unfold. She was held fast, by a sense of unease. A voice that she later, to regret, not having listened to.

Unable to concentrate, she kept pacing, slowly, around the flat. Going into each room, remembering that each had housed, for a few hours, the different elements of her life, over the past year.

Finally, Stella returned to Adam's study. He had put up the map that she had given him, for his birthday. He had put it on the right-hand wall, near the window. Here, he would see it clearly, from behind his desk. She reached out to the wooden box that she had given him. The one that housed all the memories of her. The cards that she had given him, the notes that she had written to him. She traced her finger, along the figure of the elephant, so beautifully inlaid, with mother-of-pearl. She looked at her watch. Adam would be home soon.

Stella wanted to call Edward. She needed to have his strength, about her. But she realised that this was something that she would have to go through, alone. When she heard the sound of Adam's key, in the lock, she was filled with a dread, and a misery that she could barely contain. She was unable to go toward the door, to greet him. She felt a paralysis, seemingly possessing her mind, and her limbs. She stood, quite still.

Adam, calling out Stella's name, when he came in, found her standing, in his study. She looked at him, as if she was not really seeing him. Her expression shuttered, and remote.

Stella, looking at him, saw how tired, and drawn he looked, after his journey. But she realised, that what she had to say could no longer wait.

'Adam,' she said, 'come. Sit down.' She led the way into the sitting room.

11

Adam, sitting down on the sofa, noticed that Stella did not join him. She sat in an armchair, facing him. At first, he was perplexed, then worried.

'Is something wrong, Stella?' he asked. 'Are you ill?'

'Adam,' she said, almost unable to go on, 'I'm leaving.'

'Leaving? Leaving, to go where?' he asked. 'Is this about your work?'

'No,' she said. 'No, Adam. I'm leaving here. I'm leaving you.'

Adam looked at her, not understanding. As if she were speaking, in a foreign tongue. He saw that there were tears, coursing, silently, down her face.

'Have you met someone else?' he asked quietly, his voice barely audible. 'Yes,' she said, staring down at her hands.

Adam sat in silence, for some moments, unable to speak.

'Is it someone I know, Stella?'

Stella now looked up at him. 'Yes. Yes, it is.'

'Are you going to tell me, who?'

'Edward,' she said.

'Edward?' he said. 'Edward? The friend of mine, the one you only met, a few months ago. That Edward?' Adam sounded as if in pain, as if he had, somehow, sustained a hard blow.

Stella, her head still bowed, nodded. Raising her head, she saw that Adam's eyes were dull, his face set rigid.

'I'm so sorry, Adam,' she said. 'I am so very sorry.' She could find no other words. There were no other words.

Looking at him, Stella was reminded of a time, some years ago. She had gone to stay with some friends, in County Clare, in the south of Ireland. They had gone fishing, taking the boat out onto Lough Derg. Stella, who had never fished before, was the only one with a catch, that day. It was a Perch. She looked at the fish in awe, mesmerized by its beauty. It writhed on the deck, the sunlight glinting off it. Its scales luminous. Shades of greens and blues, shimmering, as light on flowing water. She had wanted to throw the fish back into the water. But someone had stepped forward, administering the priest. As the fish stopped writhing, the colour started to drain from its scales, leaving it still and lifeless. She had cried then, as she was crying now. But this time, she was crying for Adam, and for herself. Of what had been between them. Of a life, drained of all light.

There was silence between them. Adam stunned by what had been laid before him. Seemingly, unable to comprehend. When he did speak, it was with the calm of resignation.

'Be careful, Stella. Edward is a deeply damaged person. Troubled, and dangerous. He is used to taking what he wants, discarding it when he is finished. You will see, in time, that you will be no match for him. You think that you can save him from all that. But Edward does not want to be saved. His torment, his inner turmoil, is what drives him on. It is the basis of his work.' Adam got up, pacing the room, not looking at her.

Stella could feel Adam's pain, his hurt. She felt completely helpless, in the plain sight of his misery. But she had been left with no choice. She realized that, from the first she had met Edward, she no longer belonged to herself.

Adam finally turned to look at her.
'Some homecoming, Stella,' he said. 'Some homecoming.' He shook his head, in disbelief. 'I had made such plans for us.'

The Unreal Dance

Stella got up from the armchair, moving toward him. He looked so stricken. She wanted to offer him some comfort. Adam moved away, turning his back on her. She stood still, where she was. She realized that, from now on, this is the way it was to be. The desolation that she felt was beyond measure.

'I can go and spend the night with Patricia,' she said. 'I'll come back, over the next few days, to pack.'

'You must do as you wish,' he said. 'But I'm the one who is leaving. I cannot, even bear, to think of you, or Edward. These walls are a reminder of all that we had. Everything here is a reminder of all that we could have had.'

Without another word, Adam left the room. Stella heard him, moving from room to room, gathering the things that he would need. She heard him collecting what he needed from the bathroom. She heard him go into the bedroom, packing up his clothes. Finally, she heard him go into his study. Here, for a long time, she heard nothing. And then, she heard a crash. The sound held anger, and violence. Stella did not move. Adam left, without saying goodbye.

She remained where she was for some while, unable to rouse herself. She was overcome by a tiredness, a numbness. A sad realization, that she had brought all this, to pass. When she, finally, managed to move, she walked over to Adam's study. As she stood in the doorway, she found herself, quietly sobbing. She saw that Adam had destroyed the wooden box, the one that had sat on his desk. The box, housing the memories of her. Of their time together. Stella bent down, trying to retrieve some of the pieces, thinking that somehow, it could be put back together, again. But the damage, done, was beyond repair.

Stella went and lay down on the bed. Suddenly afraid of what the future would bring. She stared into the darkness, and the darkness gazed back.

12

Stella lay on her side and watched the dawn coming up. She was still fully dressed, from the evening before. Although her limbs were chilled, and cramped, her sleep had been strangely peaceful. Her fears, of the night before, had faded. She felt a strength of resolve and purpose. The heavy weight of a burden had been put down.

She realised that she should have telephoned Edward, the night before. He would have been waiting for her call. But after the sight of first, bewilderment, then of misery, on Adam's face, she had found herself, beyond all words. This was a circumstance that had come about, from little choice. Devastating, in its impact, yet unavoidable. The premonition had been there, long before the unfolding of the story.

Stella stood, for a long time, under the shower. The hot needles of water slowly warming her aching muscles. She was glad that it was the weekend. This would give her time to organize her work and make a start on her packing. She made a pot of coffee, and sat down, to make the lists of all that had to be done. It was not yet six o'clock. She knew that she should call Edward. He would be waiting. But she needed a little more time, the look on Adam's face, still haunting her. She longed to talk to Adam. To try and explain. But it was too soon, far too soon. His pain still too raw. And what explanation would she give, for destroying what had seemed so perfect. The map of the human heart is a dangerous place to navigate. There are no boundaries, there are no signposts. It is a territory that remains unknown.

Sitting at the desk, in her study, Stella stared sightlessly, through the window, her mind not able to focus. Edward. She would telephone Edward. She needed to hear the strength, and certainty, in his voice. She reached out and dialled his number. He answered on the first ring.

'Stella?'

'I talked to Adam last night', she said. 'He's gone, Edward. He's gone.'

For some moments, Edward said nothing. He could only imagine how hard it must have hit Adam. He was filled with a sorrow, a sense of loss.

'Do you know where he's gone?' he asked.

'No. His hurt was unbearable. At first, he didn't seem able to take in what I was saying. And then, as an understanding took hold of him, the light went out of his eyes. It was replaced by a bleakness of the reality. A reality that he could not comprehend. There was no anger, only a deep bewilderment. He said that he no longer wanted to be here. That everything would be a reminder of what had been between us.'

'We had no choice, Stella. We had no choice. From first we met, that choice was taken from us. We have both lost someone. Someone so dear. Someone so dear to us both. But there are no doubts. I have never felt so certain, so sure, of anything, in my life.'

'I know', she said. 'But the damage done will always weigh heavily on me.'

'I've looked for you all my life, Stella. Until now, it's been a long and lonely journey. I feel a sense of a hope that has eluded me for so long. I'll make you so happy. I promise.'

Some years later, Stella would be reminded of these words. Words that she had been so quick to take comfort in. Wrapping them around her, careless of the outside world. Not remembering, that these were words that could heal pain, as well as inflicting it.

By late morning, Stella had prepared the work for the following week's meetings. She decided to take a walk, and perhaps stop somewhere, for lunch. She was on her way out, when the telephone rang. She hesitated, before she answered, thinking that it might be Adam. It was Patricia.

'Stella? Are you alright?' she asked. 'Have you talked to Adam?'

'I talked to him last night. A night, I'm trying hard, not to remember.'

'Shall we meet tomorrow?' Patricia asked. 'We can talk then.'

'I'd like that. I'll start on my packing, in the morning. We can have a long lunch.'

That evening, Stella went to Edward. He was waiting for her.

'Welcome home, Stella', he said, opening the door, and folding her into him, 'Welcome home.'

He poured them each a glass of wine.
'To a new beginning', he said, raising his glass. 'To our new beginning.'
'To our new beginning', Stella said, smiling. All thought of Adam having faded. Another chapter closed.

When Stella awoke, the next morning, Edward's side of the bed was empty. As she turned to look at the bedside clock, she saw a tissue wrapped parcel, on the pillow, next to her. There was a handwritten card on it. 'I hope you like this, darling. Come up to the studio, when you're awake.' Sitting up, she carefully unwrapped the paper. Inside was a robe of heavy silk. A dark, midnight blue, with a lining of grey. The robe, embroidered, with roses. From the palest of pinks, to the darkest of reds. Stella held it to the side of her face, before slipping it on. She made her way up to the studio.

She stood in the doorway, for some moments, watching Edward so completely absorbed in his work. This was a side of him that she had not seen before. Always so composed and immaculate, he was unshaven, wearing paint-covered jeans, and an oversized linen shirt. There was a vulnerability about him, a gentleness.

Edward, pausing for a moment, noticed Stella, standing in the doorway.
'You look beautiful', he said. 'Do you realize, I've never seen you, first thing in the morning?'
He walked over to her and took her hand. 'Come', he said, 'I'll make us breakfast.'

When they reached the kitchen, she saw that the table had already been laid.

'Don't look so surprised, Stella', he said, smiling. 'I'm trying to impress you.'

'I'm impressed', she said, laughing. 'I am impressed.'

Over breakfast, they discussed their plans for the day. Stella said that she would be going back to the flat, and that she had arranged to have lunch with Patricia. Edward said that he would be working.

As she was leaving, Edward handed her a set of keys for the house. He put his arms around her, holding her tight to him.

'I'll see you tonight', he said. 'I'll miss you.'

Any doubts that Stella might have had about this new life, went in that instant. She felt a happiness, and a certainty, that was beyond all measure.

Letting herself into the flat, she felt a loneliness. The sense of a loss, that she could not quite grasp. There was a lifelessness, within these walls, as if no-one lived here. As if those who had lived here, had gone out, and never come back. Leaving behind only the shadow of memories.

Patricia arrived a little after mid-day. Sensing Stella's mood, she suggested that they should go out and find somewhere to have lunch. She too, could feel the emptiness of what had once been a home.

It was with a sense of relief that they closed the front door and went into the outside. They walked for some twenty minutes, neither of them saying much. The restaurant that they had decided on, was a small, old fashioned, French bistro. Checked tablecloths, candles in wine bottles, the songs of Edith Piaf, playing in the background. It was a place that they had been coming to for some years. It had been the backdrop, for both Stella's, and Patricia's, moments of happiness, and moments of misery. It provided the comfort of the familiar.

After they had ordered their food, Patricia sat back and waited for Stella to open the conversation. She had learned, a long time ago, that there was no point in asking Stella any questions. Stella would tell her own story, in her own way, when she was ready.

When the food had been brought, and the wine had been poured, Stella started to speak.

'I know what you're wondering, Patricia. What you haven't asked. Why I would give up a life, a life so happy, a life so certain, for a man that I hardly know.' Stella, taking a sip of her wine, stared into a distance, lost in thought.

'It's quite simple', she said. 'I've fallen into a love. A love that has woken me, from a lulled state. I did love Adam. I still do. Had I not met Edward, things would have turned out differently. But I did meet Edward. I knew from that first time that I met him, there would be a change in my life. I just didn't know what.' She stopped for a while, looking, intently, down at the table. As if there were a box, full of words, in front of her. And she had to pick out the right ones, to lay out, in front of Patricia.

Patricia leant forward, putting her hand on Stella's.
'I'm not questioning what you've done, Stella, or judging you. It's just that, after all these years, you seemed to have found what you had been looking for. After the time that you had with Jack, you completely withdrew from the outside world. With Adam, you found your way back. He brought you back to a place of safety.'

'That's just it', Stella said. 'It's been a place of safety. A cocoon, a shelter. I was as a passenger, in the relationship. I know that I made Adam happy. But I now also realise, that his love for me was far greater than my love for him. There was no real balance between us. He felt too much for me. He did too much for me.'

They said nothing, for a while. Patricia, eating her food. Stella, hardly touching hers.

'You see', Stella continued, 'Adam's love, was protecting me, and shielding me, from the outside world. That sort of love will, eventually dull you. It will, gradually, change your feelings, from a love to a dependency. It gets to a point, where you have no real role, in your own life. It becomes too easy to give up all will.'

'I hadn't realised', Patricia said. 'You seemed so happy. You seemed to have found a degree of stability. A stability that you'd searched for, for so long.'

The waiter came over and cleared their plates. They ordered coffee. When the coffees were brought, Stella started to speak again.

'I know', she said, 'that I've been hit by a madness, and a blindness. Edward has stolen my heart. He has stolen me, from myself. I also know that my life with him will be an uncertain path. But for the first time, in a very long time, I feel a sense of purpose. I feel not only loved, but also much needed.'

Patricia said nothing, staring down, intently, at her coffee, as if trying to divine the future.

'When I first saw Edward's work at his exhibition', Stella said, 'I felt a sense of recognition. I could feel the loneliness, the not belonging. That feeling, that one has, between the end of a dream, and the reality of the day. That blurred, no man's land, with no outline. Nor any definition. I felt that I had gone, where he had gone. Had seen what he had seen. I suddenly, no longer, felt alone.'

Patricia was listening carefully to what Stella was saying. She noted an animation, in her face, and in her voice, that had not been there for some years.

'Since we met', Stella continued, 'there has been a change in Edward's work. A new hope. It is almost imperceptible, but it is a beginning. It is like a shoot, from a seed, fighting through dense earth, toward a light. I have done that, Patricia. I have done that. It gives me a sense of strength, a sense of power.'

'I understand', Patricia said, smiling. 'I really do.'

Stella looked at her watch. It was already late into the afternoon.

'Will you be seeing Edward this evening?' Patricia asked.

'Yes. But I have to return to the flat, first, to collect some things. Will you come back with me?'

Patricia nodded. She understood. Stella did not want to be at the flat, on her own.

13

When Stella went to Edward that evening, she was about to ring the doorbell, when she remembered that he had given her a set of keys that morning. She let herself in and called out his name.

'I'm in here, Stella', he answered. 'I'm in the kitchen.'

When Stella went into the kitchen, she was astonished. Edward was standing by the cooker, stirring something, in a pot. The table had been laid. Tapered cream candles, in pewter holders, had been lit. A bottle of wine, on a silver salver, had been opened. There were dark green, crystal, wine glasses, and folded, linen napkins. There was a platter of roasted peppers, and tomatoes, on the vine. Beside this, a bowl of fat queen olives, in oil.

Edward, noting her surprise, smiled at her, with some amusement.

'Even struggling artists, have to eat', he laughed.'

Stella went over to where he was standing and wrapped her arms around him. Edward put down the spoon that he was holding and kissed the top of her head.

'Sit down, Stella', he said. 'I'll be with you, in a minute.'

Stella sat down and watched Edward. He poured the sauce that he had been stirring, into a small bowl, and placed it on the table. As he opened the oven door, the room was filled with the scent of garlic and rosemary. There was a dish of small, baked goat's cheeses, studded with sprigs of rosemary. There was a hot loaf of garlic bread.

Edward poured out the wine and sat down.

'This a feast, Edward', Stella said. 'This is a veritable feast.'

Edward smiled but said nothing. When he finally spoke, it was with a serious note.

'This week is going to be difficult for you, Stella. Leaving a place that you've lived in, been happy in, is never easy. I'm going to do my best to make you happy here. You know I will. I think that, once you have moved in, properly, then the shadows will start to fade.'

Stella listened to him, making no comment, waiting for him to continue.

'As you know', he went on, 'I've got an exhibition to prepare for, in the New Year. Although I'll be working here, there will be days when we'll only just cross paths. And so, I thought that, in a couple of weeks, we could go away, for a few days. I have a friend, a writer, who has a house on the Dorset coast. He built it, some years ago, as some sort of retreat. It's really, quite beautiful there. I thought that it was time that we got to know each other properly.'

Stella smiled at that. She wondered if one could, ever, get to know someone, as complex as Edward, properly.

'I'd love to', she said. 'It sounds wonderful.'

'And', Edward continued, 'I've had a new telephone line, installed in your study. It should be connected tomorrow. Let me know what shelving you want, and I can build those this week.'

Stella reached over and took his hand.

'Thank you', she said, 'thank you. You're making life so easy for me. I'll have to get to the flat, early, tomorrow. I want to be there before Mrs. Hughes, the cleaning lady, arrives. I'll have to explain why there are boxes everywhere. And why, there are piles of clothes on the bed.'

'Have you heard from Adam?' Edward asked.

'No', Stella said, 'no.'

The mention of Adam's name brought a chill to them both, reminding them of their own happiness, and his misery. The price, that had had, to be paid.

'We both miss him', Edward said, reading Stella's mind. 'It's not something that will ever go away.'

Stella, looked down at the table, wordlessly. Not realizing, as yet, the true cost of the price, that would have to be paid. That would come later.

14

It was a little before nine o'clock, the next morning, when Stella reached the flat. She made a pot of coffee and waited for Mrs. Hughes to arrive. She heard the sound of the keys, in the front door, and went to meet her, in the hallway.

'I've just made some coffee', Stella said. 'I thought we might have it, in the kitchen.'

Mrs. Hughes followed her, noticing the cardboard boxes in the living room. She did not remark on these.

Stella poured them both a cup of coffee. They sat at the table.

'This is very difficult for me', Stella said. 'I'm sure that you must have noticed all the boxes. Adam, and I, we're separating. I'll be moving out in the next few days.'

Stella noted the look of complete astonishment on the woman's face.

'Adam is not living here at the moment', she went on, 'he'll move back in, when I've gone.'

Mrs. Hughes sat looking at her hands, for a few moments.

'I'm very sorry about all this, Stella', she said. 'I really am. I've been with Adam for a long time. I'd never seen him so happy.'

Stella felt close to tears. The thought of Adam's misery, the thought of his coming back, to an empty home, hit her, almost as a physical blow. It was some moments before she realised that the telephone was ringing. It was Adam. She barely recognised his voice. It was dull, devoid of any emotion.

'I was hoping to find you', he said. 'I've accepted an assignment in Washington. I'll be gone for at least six months. I need to come and collect some things. I'll be leaving in about a week. I think that it would be best, if we could arrange a time when you're not there.'

'Adam...' Stella started to cry, softly, 'Adam...'

'No, Stella. No. There is nothing left to be said.' With that, he rang off.

Stella stood staring, at the telephone receiver, in her hand. It was as if she was willing his voice to come back, on the line. She wanted to tell him how desperately sorry she was. How she had never meant for any of this to happen. But the line was dead.

When Stella went back into the kitchen, she saw that Mrs. Hughes was waiting for her.

'Stella, my dear', she said, noticing how tired, and drawn Stella suddenly looked, 'why don't I start folding your clothes, and putting them on the bed. You can carry on organising the packing, in your study.'

Stella thanked her. She was grateful for this help and understanding. She felt better, having someone there with her.

It was midday before Stella stopped, her files and books packed, and labelled, so that she would have easy access to everything. She went to find Mrs. Hughes. She was in the bedroom. Stella saw that her clothes had been folded and placed into piles. Her side of the cupboard, now empty. Soon, it would seem, as if she had never been here. She felt a sadness that was beyond measure.

'Mrs. Hughes, shall we go out for lunch?' Stella asked.

'I'd love to, my dear. But please stop calling me Mrs. Hughes. Mary. It's Mary.'

After a quick lunch, they returned to the flat. By early afternoon, the packing was finished. Mary said that she would return, the next day, to do the cleaning.

'Good luck, my dear', she said to Stella. 'I do hope that you'll be happy.'

'Thank you', Stella said. 'And thank you for your help today.'

When Mary had left, Stella telephoned Edward. He sensed straight away that there was something wrong. She told him about the conversation with Adam. He understood.

'How far are you along with your packing?' he asked.

'I've finished. Everything is ready.'

'Good', he said. 'I'll be with you soon. It may take a few trips, but I think it best that we move everything tonight.'

Stella felt a sudden rush of relief. She had had a haunting sense of loneliness, and isolation, all day. She went into the kitchen and poured herself a large brandy. She sat at the kitchen table and waited for Edward to arrive. She no longer belonged here.

Edward arrived, shortly after. Stella was ready. He did not comment on the pallor of her skin, nor her tear-stained eyes. He held her, for a very long time, stroking her hair gently, away from her face, as one would, of that of a child. He made three journeys, from the flat, to his house, taking her with him, each time. He did not want to leave her, on her own. As they were leaving, for the last time, Stella took the house keys from her bag, and locking the door, from the outside, dropped them through the letterbox. As they hit the wood of the polished floor, there was the sound of a finality. Of the end, of a no return.

Edward took her, by the hand, and led her to the car. The journey, to the house, was a silent one. Both lost, in their own thoughts. Both thinking of what had been done, and what was to be done. Both realising, that the line that had been crossed, would affect them, forever.

15

The week that followed passed quickly. Stella would spend an hour, or so organising her day's work, and would then go out to attend meetings with the various charities involved in that autumn's event. Each evening, she would return, to find Edward building, and painting, the shelves, in her study. He would then prepare dinner, while she unpacked the boxes that were lined up, against one wall. A pattern had emerged. Thinking about this, Stella realised how quickly a pattern can emerge. In the space of a few weeks, she had exchanged the pattern of one life, replacing it with the pattern of another.

It was toward the end of this week that Stella ran into Adam. She was walking down a small side street, in central London. She had just finished a meeting and was making her way to another. It was here that she came, face to face, with him. He looked at her for a moment, seeming, at first, not to recognise her. His face was pale. Thinner than she remembered. His eyes, as he looked at her, quite dead. They stood, staring at each other. Two strangers.

'I see', he said, with some bitterness, 'that you managed to remove all traces of our life together, from the flat. All except the map, the one on my study wall. I'll pack that up, and have it sent on to you.'

'I want you to keep that, Adam', Stella said. 'It was my birthday present, to you.'

'I remember. My birthday present. I marvel at the fact that you managed, to find the time, to look for anything, while you were seeing another man. I must say, Stella, I'm truly impressed by your powers of deception.'

Stella was silent. She waited for Adam to continue.

'If you had left me, for a complete stranger, it would have been bad enough. But no. You had to choose someone whose life was so deeply entwined, with mine.'

Stella put out a hand, to touch his arm. Adam stepped back.

'Don't, Stella', he said. 'And for God's sake, don't try the "let's be friends" bit. Friendships are fragile things. They're based on a degree of honesty, a degree of loyalty, a degree of respect. These are things that I haven't had from you. I'd like to say that I wish you well. I'd like to say that I wish you happiness. But I can't.' With that, he walked on.

Stella was left shaken, unable to move. When she finally looked around, Adam had disappeared.

That evening, when she returned to the house, she was unusually silent. If Edward noticed, he said nothing. Stella did not mention her encounter with Adam. That night, her dreams were troubled. She dreamt that she was in the park. There were hundreds of children, sailing their model boats, on the pond. They all had their backs to her. When they turned around, she saw that some of their faces were like Edward's, and some of their faces, like Adam's. She walked toward them, but they turned away from her and walked away. This dream stayed on her mind, for some days.

That morning, Stella told Edward that she could take a few days off, at the end of the following week. He was delighted.

'You're going to love it', he said. 'You're really going to love it. Long walks, on the beach. Suppers, by the open fire.'

'Okay. Okay. You've sold it to me', Stella laughed. 'I won't want to come back.'

Edward looked at her curiously, a slight shadow, passing over his face.

'Oh. We always have to come back, Stella. We always have to come back.'

These words brought a chill to Stella. As if they had touched, on a long forgotten, on a long buried, memory. If she felt a premonition of things to come, she did not heed it.

'Edward', she said, 'I'm meeting Patricia for lunch. I think that it's about time you two met. What do you think?'

'Why don't you ask her over, this weekend? I can wear a paint splattered smock, a beret, and act out the character of an eccentric artist.'

'I don't think you need a smock, or a beret, for that, Edward. I think you do pretty well, as you are', she laughed.

Stella had been looking forward to her lunch with Patricia for some days. The few telephone conversations that they had had, had been brief. They met, at the same French restaurant that they had eaten at, two weeks before.

Patricia, arriving a few minutes late, noted that Stella looked quite radiant. The look that comes from the first burst of love. This look only briefly shadowed, when Stella told her about her encounter with Adam.

After the menus had been brought and they had both ordered, they both started to speak at once.

'You first', Patricia said. 'Tell me everything.'

'Before I start', Stella laughed, 'we'd like you to come over this weekend. How about dinner on Saturday night?'

'I'd love that. But I must say, I do feel a little nervous.'

'Don't be. I know everything will be fine. Anyway, you can't be as nervous as he is. He was already planning the meal, when I left this morning.'

'He's going to cook the meal?' Patricia asked, with some astonishment.

'Oh, yes. I've managed to train him, in the short time that I've been there.'

'I don't know how you do it, Stella. I honestly don't. I've never even managed to get a man to make me a cup of tea. Let alone a meal.'

They were both silent. Both thinking about the times that Patricia had, in the past, gone around to have dinner with Stella and Adam. How he had

The Unreal Dance

left them to talk, while he prepared the meal. Those were times, gone. Times that would never be repeated.

'Are you happy, Stella? Really happy?' Patricia asked.

'I am', Stella replied. 'Beyond all measure.'

After they had left the restaurant, they walked, in silence, for about ten minutes, before going their separate ways. Patricia went back to her office, and Stella made her way back to the house.

On her way back, Stella stopped at a small Italian delicatessen. Here she bought a loaf of olive bread, slices of Parma ham, artichoke hearts in olive oil, and a dozen, dark purple, ripe figs. She then went to the flower shop, buying cream and deep blue, long stemmed freesias. She took a taxi back to the house.

When she let herself in, the house was quiet. Stella had seen Edward's car outside, and realized that he was in the studio, working. There was a note on the kitchen table. It said that he was upstairs, and that he would be down, around seven o'clock. It also said that a package had arrived for her, and that he had put it in her study. Curious, she went upstairs to look.

The package was leaning against the wall. It was wrapped in heavy, brown paper. It had her name and address on the front. The writing was in Adam's hand. It was the framed map that she bought him for his birthday. He had returned it. Stella carried it upstairs and placed it at the back of one of her cupboards. She was never to unwrap it.

Deeply upset, she went downstairs and sat staring out into the garden, for some time. Adam had removed any memory of her, from within his walls.

Stella went into the kitchen, putting away the food that she had bought, and placing the flowers into vases. She realized that Edward would have recognized Adam's handwriting. But when he came down later, he made no mention of this.

On Saturday morning, Stella came downstairs to find Edward sitting at the kitchen table, with several sheets of paper, neatly placed in front of him. Each sheet of paper had some sort of list on it. She asked him what he was doing. He said that he was writing out various menus, with a list of the ingredients that each would require. Stella, knowing Patricia, could decide which menu to choose.

'I want to impress her', Edward said.

'Well, you've impressed me. You've done all the cooking, since I moved here', she laughed.

'Don't laugh, Stella. When we come back from Dorset, you'll be in charge of the kitchen. I'll be working long days, and some long nights. By the time the exhibition opens, you'll be begging me to get back to the stove.'

'We'll see', Stella said. 'We'll see.'

'I want Patricia to like me', he said, on a serious note. 'I know how important she is to you.

'Of course she'll like you.'

'And suppose she doesn't?' he asked, quietly.

'Then, you'll just have to pack up all your belongings and leave', she laughed. 'Now, let me have a look at all these menus, and we can decide.'
When Edward left, to go to the shops, Stella cleared the breakfast dishes and tidied up the downstairs. She found that she was as nervous as Edward.

Patricia arrived, a little before seven o'clock, that evening. She walked into a house that was heady from the scent of flowers, and the warm fragrance of cooking. It was Edward who opened the door to her. They stood on the doorstep looking at each other, for a long moment. Then Edward took her hand and led her into the house.

'Come and sit in the garden, Patricia. I'll get you a drink. Stella, will be down in a few minutes.'

Patricia smiled. She realized Stella had wanted her, and Edward, to have a little time on their own.

Edward went into the kitchen and came out carrying a bottle of chilled white wine, and three glasses. Patricia followed him out, into a large walled garden. The walls of the garden, covered in cream and yellow, climbing roses,

The Unreal Dance

entwined with each other. The large pots, filled with jasmine and Mexican orange blossom. The air was heavy, with their perfume. Patricia felt, as if she had stepped into, a small paradise.

Edward filled the three glasses with the wine. He heard Stella, coming down the steps, into the garden. She smiled at him. He smiled back. After a brief toast, Edward returned to the kitchen, saying that dinner would be ready, in about half an hour.

After Edward had left, Patricia turned to Stella, raising her glass.

'To a great happiness, Stella', she said. 'To a magical future.'

Stella, taking a sip of her wine, did not notice the slight hesitation, in Patricia's voice.

They had dinner in the dining room. Stella had taken great care in setting the table. A bowl of roses, picked from the garden, was placed at the centre. There were long, tapered candles, at each end. The lamps, around the room, were dimmed. The meal that Edward had prepared, quite delicious. Although, saying little, Edward was courteous, and charming. But Patricia felt a sense of disquiet, a sense of unease. Every time that she looked up, she saw Edward looking at Stella, with a focus, with an intensity. She wondered, to herself, if this was a love, or an obsession. Behind the façade, she could sense a troubled man, a damaged man. She remembered Stella's life, with Jack. She was reminded that damaged people could, sometimes, cause great damage. She hoped that she was wrong. There was nothing that she could have said to Stella, at the time. After all, it was just a feeling. Later, much later, she wished that she had voiced her misgivings. But by then, it would prove to be too late. Sometimes, we do not see what we should see. And sometimes, this blindness will not let us go, where we should go.

16

On Monday morning, Edward introduced Stella to Frieda.

Frieda was a Polish woman, who came in three times a week, to clean the house. Edward explained that he had given her two weeks off, so that Stella could settle in, at her own pace.

When Frieda came in, she was surprised by the change in the house. There were flowers, in vases, there was an opened book, lying face down, on a table, there was a notebook, with a pen beside it, on the sideboard. The house, which she had, so beautifully kept over the years, had been transformed into a home. There had been many women in Edward's life, but none had, before, moved in. Edward had always said that he liked to live alone. He, too, seemed transformed. He looked so happy. There was an air of playfulness about him, when he talked to Stella. This was a side of him that she had not seen before. She was pleased. She asked Stella if she had any special instructions. Stella, smiling at her, said that she had none, other than, she would clean her own study. She also told Frieda that she and Edward would be going away for a few days, from mid-week.

On Wednesday morning, Stella awoke early. The thought of going away that day, filled her with the excitement of a child. She had packed the night before. They would buy food, from the nearby village, when they arrived.

When they got into the car, Stella turned to Edward, and cupping his face, in her hands, kissed him, deeply.

'What was that for?' he laughed.

'For making me so happy', she said.

The Unreal Dance

Although the journey was a long one, the time passed quickly. The day was warm, the skies clear. Stella spent, most of the time, staring out of the window, watching the towns, and the villages, go by. At one point, she was reminded of all the plans that she had made, with Adam. The plans of spending some time away. The plans, that had come to nothing. A shadow passed over her. But it was soon gone.

It was just after mid-day, when they arrived. They had stopped at the village, to shop. The house, built on high stilts, stood on the beach. It stood on its own. The only other houses were a long distance away.

Edward unpacked the car and then showed Stella around. The living room was large, with a stone fireplace at one end. There were sliding glass doors, almost as a glass wall, leading to a veranda that ran the length of it. The view was quite breathtaking. Edward showed her to the bedroom, where they would be sleeping. The second bedroom was used as an office.

'Lucien', he explained, 'bought this house, a little over a year after his wife died. In that year, he almost went mad with grief. He almost drank himself, to death. Then one day, when he was researching, for a book that he was writing, he found this house. It saved his life. Now, he comes down, when he first starts a book, and then when he is finishing it.'

While Stella unpacked, Edward set the fire for later that evening. When he had finished, he suggested that they go out for lunch.

'There's a small pub, a short way away', he said. 'We can reach it by way of the beach.'

The publican, when they got there, greeted Edward, warmly, and showed them to a corner table.

Stella wondered how often Edward had come down, in the past. And, with how many different women. But she quickly put these thoughts aside. Jealousy, she thought wryly, was truly the sting in the tail of love. Something that was always there, but had to be, carefully avoided. She knew that this was never easy.

After their lunch, they took a long walk, before returning to the house. Although the day was still warm, Edward lit the fire, opening the doors to the balcony. He put out two chairs. He took out his sketch pad, and Stella her book. They sat, side by side, each holding the other's hand. For a long time, they sat in silence, looking out, toward the fathoms of the sea.

'Look at us, Stella', he said. 'Look at us. We've already become, like a pair, of old slippers, sitting in comfort, one beside the other. This is how I always want to be. This is how I want us to grow old together.'

At that moment, a cloud appeared, seemingly out of nowhere, obscuring the sun. Stella said nothing. She tightened her grip on Edward's hand.

The days that followed, passed, far too quickly. There were long walks. There were leisurely meals. Edward capturing memories in his drawings. Stella, storing memories, for a later time. These would be days to remember.

Then, on their last night, before returning home, things changed. They were sitting on the veranda, after they had eaten. The light, from the fire, giving a warmth to the fading light. Edward, not turning to her, still looking out, toward the darkening sea, spoke to her, in a voice she barely recognized. There was an edge to it. There was a coldness. Stella, unprepared, was taken aback.

'The package that came for you, last week, was from Adam. I could not help but notice his handwriting. Are you in contact with him?'

'I wouldn't call it contact', Stella said, astonished that he should, only now, bring this up. 'It was a present that I had given him, for his birthday. I ran into him at the beginning of last week. He said that he didn't want it. That he wanted nothing, to remind him of me. That he would return it.'

Edward was silent, for some moments, seeming not to have heard anything that she had said.

'You saw Adam, and you didn't think about mentioning it, to me?' he asked, his voice now harsh. 'Is there a story behind this, Stella? Are we going to start our lives together, with secrets?'

'No Edward', Stella said quietly, 'there will be no secrets. My encounter with Adam left me upset. Talking to you, about it, would have attached an importance to it, that it didn't have. I really just wanted to forget about the whole thing.'

Edward stood up, going into the house. He came back, carrying two glasses of brandy and a packet of cigarettes. Stella watched, as he lit, one of the cigarettes. His face tense, in the flame of the lighter.

'I'm sorry', he said, his voice barely audible. 'It's just that, all this, is new to me. You must realize, I've never felt anything like this, before.'

Stella said nothing. The jealousy that love brings, in its wake, is inevitable. The destruction that that jealousy brings, in its wake, is inevitable. She had seen an anger in Edward that had frightened her. She knew that the depth of anger never goes away. That it is, never very far away. She would be mindful of this.

The next morning, they left early. Edward was relaxed, his outburst, of the night before, seemingly forgotten. The journey back home was quiet but not tense.

When they reached the house, Edward turned to Stella and pulled her toward him, wrapping his arms tightly around her.

'Let's put off, our blissful domesticity, until tomorrow', he joked. 'Let's go out and wander the streets. We can walk. We can go to the cinema. We can do anything that you want.'

'Come on, then', Stella said, laughing, 'let's go quickly, before you change your mind, and disappear up into your studio.'

As they let themselves into the house later, the telephone was ringing. Stella went into the kitchen, while Edward took the call. After a brief conversation, he came to her.

'Stella, my darling', he said. 'The honeymoon is over. It's time to meet my family. That was my mother, on the telephone. We've been asked, or rather summoned, for lunch, next Sunday. I said that I would ask you and call her back. Is it alright with you?'

'Of course it is, Edward. I shall look forward to it.'

'Don't be too hasty, Stella. Don't be too hasty.' With that, he went to the telephone, to call his mother back.

17

The next morning, Stella only saw Edward briefly, when he came downstairs for a cup of coffee. He had been working, in his studio, since just after dawn. He asked her about her plans for the day.

'It's Monday, Edward', she said. 'I usually spend Mondays, on my own.'

'What do you do, all day?' he asked her, smiling.

'I wander through town, looking through bookshops, looking through antique shops, finding somewhere to have lunch. It's something I've done for years. I'll get us a picnic supper. That way, you can eat whenever you stop work.'

Edward, having drunk his coffee, gave her a brief kiss and made his way up the stairs. She could see that he was distracted, already lost in his work.

Stella poured herself a second cup of coffee, and decided to call Patricia, to see if she was free, for lunch. She was. She made a list, for all the things that she had to buy, and left.

The day was dull, but dry. Stella walked for over two hours, going down small side streets, stopping at shops, buying nothing. Looking at her watch, she realised that it was almost time to meet Patricia. She made her way to a restaurant, near Patricia's office, arriving a little early. She was shown to a table, by the window. Here, looking out, lost in her thoughts, she did not notice Patricia, until she sat down, opposite her.

'Penny for them.' Patricia laughed. 'Although, they look as if they might be worth a lot more!'

'Sorry', Stella said, 'sorry. I've been walking for miles and feel a little exhausted. Let's order. I'm starving.'

After the food had been ordered and the wine brought, Patricia sat back, and searched Stella's face, intently. Although she still looked happy, there was a hesitancy about her. An uncertainty that had not been there, the last time that she had seen her.

'Tell me, about your week away, Stella', she said. 'I want to know every little detail.'

'Surely not, every detail', she said, smiling.' Not in a public place!'

'You know what I mean', Patricia replied. 'You know exactly what I mean.'

'It was absolutely wonderful. The house overlooked the sea. We took long walks. Our evenings were spent quietly. Talking. Finding out about each other. It has been a difficult time for both of us. Always being careful, to avoid the subject of Adam. They have been close since they were young boys. It is not an easy situation. In our different ways, we both miss him.'

Patricia listened, in silence. Something was troubling Stella.

'And did the subject of Adam come up?' she asked.

'Yes. It was, on our last night, there. I let slip that I had run into Adam, the week before. The change, in Edward, was both sudden, and quite frightening. There was a depth of anger in him. A depth of jealousy. I saw a side to him that left me shaken.'

Patricia, taking in Stella's words, was not surprised. She had seen a shadow of this, in Edward, when she had had dinner with them, before they went away. But she was not going to voice her misgivings. She chose her words carefully.

'Edward's behaviour is not unnatural, Stella. For the both of you, this love affair has been impulsive and explosive. There has been no period of adjustment. The man that you once loved, is his lifelong friend. He has given that up, for you. If he should ever lose you, then he will be left with nothing.

He is not, as yet, certain, of you. There has not been enough time for that. Behind his façade of strength, Edward is a vulnerable man.'

Stella reached out, covering Patricia's hand, with hers.

'Thank you', she said. 'You always manage to put things into perspective, for me. You always manage to clear the chaos of my thoughts.'

After the lunch, Stella walked Patricia back to her office. She then started to make her way home, stopping at the shops, on the way, to buy food and flowers. It was mid-afternoon, when she arrived home. Edward was sitting at the kitchen table, reading the newspaper. He got up and kissed her.

'Did you have a good day?' he asked. 'What did you do?'

'I walked, a great deal. More than I meant to. And then I had lunch with Patricia.'

'Well, I'm glad to see you. I missed you, while you were gone. I'm going to work for another couple of hours. I'll be down for dinner.' He kissed her again, before taking the stairs to the studio.

Stella spent the next few hours arranging the flowers and preparing the dinner. She placed the chicken, in a dish, on a bed of thickly sliced red onions. She tucked lemon quarters around it. She tossed new potatoes into olive oil and arranged these, in the same dish. She picked herbs, from the garden, to go on the salad. She placed the dish, with the chicken, in the oven. She set the table. When she stopped, she was hit by a strange realization. She had done these exact same things, these exact same meals, for so many different people. She had slipped into others' lives, she had slipped into others' homes, each time, taking what had been offered. She wondered if she had ever given anything back. Other than loss. Other than unhappiness.

When Edward came down, Stella held on to him tightly. She hoped that this time, there would be no hurt. That this time, there would be no damage.

Over dinner, Stella asked Edward's advice about her flat.

'I don't know whether to rent out my flat, or to sell it', she said. 'What do you think, Edward?'

The Unreal Dance

'That, Stella, is entirely your decision. But I don't want you to have somewhere that you can run to, every time that we have an argument.'

'Are we going to have many of those?' she asked, smiling.

'Oh yes. About how much milk you put in my tea. About', he said, pointing toward the living room, 'the fact that you've taken over my favourite armchair. All sorts of important things.'

'Okay. You've made up my mind', she laughed. 'I've decided to sell it.'

Edward looked relieved. This was a commitment that he had not thought, she was, as yet, prepared to make.

Sunday arrived. Both Stella and Edward, working steadily all week. Edward, realizing how anxious Stella was, about meeting his family, stopped work early on Saturday afternoon. He made various suggestions for things to do, for the rest of the day. They went out for an early dinner and, returning, spent the rest of Saturday evening both curled up, on the sofa, watching old films.

'They're my family', Edward said, over breakfast on Sunday morning. 'I don't see much of them. But I'm afraid I'm saddled with them.'

'Will your sister, Grace, be there?' Stella asked.

She saw a shadow pass over Edward's face.

'I'm not sure', he said. 'But I can't imagine her passing up on a chance to inspect you.'

18

Edward's parents lived outside a small town, in Gloucestershire. As they approached the town, he glanced at Stella. Her face was set, with anxiety. He suggested that they should stop for a coffee, before going on. Stella smiled at him, in gratitude. The journey after, to the house, was not a long one.

The house was reached, through imposing and elaborate iron gates. The long wide driveway, walled with tall poplar trees, on either side. The house, itself, was large. It had leaded windows throughout and two turrets, one on either side. This was a house, Stella would later learn, that held many dark corners and many dark secrets.

The front door was opened to them by a plump, elderly man, with a pince-nez and a shock of white hair. Stella looked from him, to Edward, with some surprise. She could see no resemblance between the two. Edward, noticing Stella's expression, laughed out.

'This is Mr. Dawlish', he explained. 'He and his wife have been looking after this house for as long as I remember.'

'Welcome, Stella', Mr. Dawlish said. He turned to Edward. 'It's good to see you, Edward. We don't see you often enough. Your parents are waiting for you, in the drawing room.' With that, he led them through.

The drawing room was both large and imposing. Its grandeur, overwhelming. It looked untouched, unlived in. There would be no comfort to be had here. Edward, placing his hand on the small of Stella's back, guided her in. She found herself facing two unsmiling people. Edward introduced them.

'This is my mother, Angela,' he said to Stella, 'and my father, Magnus.'

Neither offered a greeting. It was as if a stranger had wandered into their house, by mistake. Stella, feeling quite unnerved, stepped forward, holding out her hand. The handshakes were brief and dry. Devoid of any warmth. She looked at Edward's mother. Angela was a faded beauty. Her pale blue eyes, looking at Stella, held no expression. They held no curiosity. Edward's father, Magnus, was not unlike a caricature of a country squire. Handmade brown brogues, dark corduroy trousers and a tweed jacket. There was, about him, a faint scent of cologne, mixed with that of whiskey and cigars.

At this point, Mr. Dawlish, came in. He told them that lunch would be ready, in half an hour. He then went over to the sideboard, where a tray of bottles and glasses had been laid out, to mix the drinks. If he noticed anything strange, about the almost frozen tableau, made up of the four people in the drawing room, he did not remark on it to himself. He had been with this family for a long time. Very little surprised him now.

'Your sister will be joining us for lunch, Edward', Angela said. 'She's driving over, from a friend's house, nearby. I do hope she's not going to be late.'

'She's always late, my dear', Magnus said, addressing his wife. 'She's always late.'

Throughout all this, Edward had remained at Stella's side. His hand still on the small of her back, as if giving her support. He could feel her discomfort. He knew that she would be comparing the warmth of Adam's parents, with that of the coldness of his own. He was not looking forward to Grace's arrival. The presence of his sister would really complete the picture.

Lunch was served, in a formal, high ceilinged dining room. The leaded windows looking out onto manicured lawns. The light from the windows, shone onto the silver cutlery and onto the crystal glasses. Five, high backed chairs, had been arranged at one end of the table. The food was brought in by Mr. and Mrs. Dawlish. Mrs. Dawlish was a tall thin woman, with an impassive face. She greeted Stella briefly, and then she turned to Edward. Here, Stella was astonished to see the change in her. Her face had lit up with a love, with a warmth.

Edward, got up from the table, and went over to Mrs. Dawlish.

'Hallo Danvers', he said, giving her a warm hug.

'Don't be so cheeky, Edward. I was rather hoping that you'd get better, as you grew older. But I see that nothing's changed.'

Edward took her by the hand and led her over to where Stella was sitting.

'This is Stella', he said to her. 'The light of my life.'

Mrs. Dawlish looked at Stella closely, for a time. Then she smiled. She could see that, at last, Edward was happy. It was, at this moment, that Grace arrived. She stood, framed in the doorway, her eyes sweeping the room. Her entrance was like that of an actor, walking onto a stage, ready to take their part. All eyes were on her.

'You're on time', her mother said, surprised. 'You're actually, on time.'

'It's a special occasion, mother', Grace replied. 'When do you remember, the last time, that Edward brought anyone home?'

There was a silence around the table. Her parents remembered the last time that Edward had brought anyone home. How could they ever forget? The last person that Edward had brought home, had been Lydia. The woman, he had later married. The woman, he had later divorced. The woman, no one ever spoke of. But all that had been a long time ago.

Grace briefly greeted her parents. She then went over to Edward, and placing a possessive hand on his shoulder, turned to Stella. She looked at Stella, with a scrutiny, with a curiosity, with an intensity. As if Stella were a rare insect, being looked at, under a microscope.

'It's good to meet you', she said, her eyes unsmiling. 'Perhaps, we could arrange to have lunch soon. Just the two of us. Get to know each other.'

'That would be lovely', Stella said. 'I'll look forward to it.'

Grace sat down, and the lunch was served. This was to be the lull before the storm.

'Edward. How's your friend, Adam?' Magnus asked. 'I often see his by-lines, in the magazine that he works for. And in a couple of the broadsheets as well. Clever chap.'

Edward froze. He had not anticipated this. He should have.

'I don't see a great deal of him', Edward replied. 'He travels rather a lot.'

Grace turned to Stella again, looking at her intently.

'Have you met Adam yet?' she asked her. Not waiting for a reply, she went on. 'I think you'd like him. I really do. He spent most of his time here, as a boy. He, and Edward were quite inseparable. A secret society of two. Then after…..', she stopped suddenly, unable to continue. Her mind, gazing into the past.

Edward, sitting almost paralysed beside Stella, reached out his hand, under the table and held on to hers. In the event, Stella was saved from making any sort of a reply. Mr. Dawlish came in, saying that Grace was wanted on the telephone. When Grace returned, the subject of Adam was not brought up again. As soon as lunch was finished, Edward looked at his watch and said that he and Stella would have to leave. He would have to get back to work on a painting that he had started. The leave taking was formal, with no promises to return soon. With only Mr. and Mrs. Dawlish coming to the front door, to see them off.

The journey home was a silent one. Both, beginning to fully realise, the impact of what they had done. Both, beginning to fully realise the extent, to which, their happiness had been built on another's misery.

When they arrived home, Edward turned to Stella, and placing his hands on her shoulder, looked at her for a long while.

'I'm so sorry, Stella', he said. 'I should have thought…..'

'No. Edward. We should have, both thought. The subject of Adam was bound to come up, sooner or later. It was inevitable.'
Edward, a bleak look in his eyes, let go of Stella and climbed the stairs, up to his studio. He did not come to bed that night. This was a pattern that would be followed, over the next few days. Stella left alone, with her own thoughts. Edward left alone, with his. It was the weekend, before Edward was ready to talk.

'Stella', he said, over breakfast, on Saturday morning, 'I must see, Adam. I must talk to him.'

'He's on an assignment in Washington, Edward. He said that he would be gone for at least six months.'

'Well, I'll telephone him later. There has to be some sort of peace.'

'Peace for whom?' Stella asked, quietly. 'Peace for whom?'

Later, that day, when Edward finally managed to get hold of him, Adam's voice was polite, but cold. He made it quite clear that he did not want to talk to Edward. That he had no intention of easing Edward's conscience. Edward was left with nothing, but a handful of dust.

The Unreal Dance

19

It was a few weeks later, after the lunch with Edward's parents, that Grace telephoned Stella, asking her if they could meet. Although hesitant, Stella agreed. There was little choice. She could not refuse to see Edward's sister, however reluctant she was. She had felt uncomfortable when she first met Grace. She felt uncomfortable now.

That evening, over dinner, Stella mentioned her conversation with Grace, to Edward.

'Be careful, Stella', he said. 'Be very careful. Grace can cause a great deal of damage. It's what she's good at. She has a talent for bringing about unhappiness. And then, taking pleasure from that unhappiness. It gives her a sense of power.'

At a later time, Stella was to remember these words. But by then, it was too late. It was far too late.

It was the following week, when Stella telephoned Grace. They arranged to have lunch the next day. Stella, telling Edward about this arrangement, noted that he was quiet. Not saying anything, this time. Only his eyes, showing a disquiet.

Grace had chosen the restaurant that they were to meet at. It was not somewhere that Stella had been to before. Not wanting to be late, she found that in fact, she was half an hour too early. She sat down at the table, which had been reserved and ordered a glass of wine. She felt apprehensive and unprepared. She did not notice Grace, until she was standing next to the table. When Stella looked up, she found that she was staring into Grace's eyes.

Eyes that were the mirror of Edward's. Something that she did not remember, from the last they met.

The menus were brought, the food ordered, a bottle of wine placed on the table. Grace sat back in her chair, a curious expression on her face. With a dull premonition, Stella knew what was coming. Grace went straight to the point.

'How did you meet my brother, Stella?' she asked.

'I met him at the opening night of his exhibition, earlier this year. I went with a friend.'

'If you went with a friend, then that friend would have to be close to Edward. He is quite peculiar about who attends his first nights. He always has been.'

Grace waited for Stella to answer, a strange look in her eyes. A look of anticipation. She sat, poised as a cat, looking on at its prey.

Stella, taking her time, realised that she would have to choose her words carefully.

'I went with Adam', she said.

'Adam? Adam Cavanaugh?' she asked, not a little surprised. 'And how do you know him?'

Stella, hesitating, knew that she had no choice. The story had to be told. When she had finished telling it, she looked at Grace, with an expression that brooked no further questions.

Grace had sat quietly. Listening intently. Unable to believe what she was hearing.

'Bloody hell, Stella', she finally said. 'Bloody hell. Poor Adam. Poor Edward. You have made a mess of things, haven't you? You really have.'

Stella, having always acknowledged her part in the pain and the hurt that had come about, was astonished that Grace would place all the blame, with her. That she had absolved Edward of any participation, of any responsibility. But then, Stella was the outsider. She would always be the outsider.

Returning home, she found Edward downstairs, waiting for her. Close to tears, she went to him, holding onto him tightly. She told him about the conversation at the lunch. Edward showed no surprise. He knew Grace well.

'It had to happen, Stella', he said, trying to calm her. 'It had to happen. Better now, than later.'

20

It was one evening, toward the end of summer, when Grace came back into their lives. There had been no contact since the lunch Stella had had with her. Looking back, it was to prove to be the start of a new chapter. A chapter that would have been best left unwritten.

Stella was in the kitchen preparing the evening meal. These meals had become simple affairs, quick to put together, as Stella never knew when Edward would be coming down from his studio. She looked at the kitchen counter. Everything was ready. Small bowls were arranged in a row. A bowl of chopped flat leaf parsley, a bowl of chopped garlic, a bowl of small plump scallops, their corals separated. Beside these stood a bottle of dark green olive oil, a jar of dried chilies, two lemons halved. She would pan fry all these while she cooked the pasta. The table was set, the wine opened. The evening was warm, the French doors to the garden open.

Stella was on her way to the garden, to pick a few roses for the table, when the doorbell rang. It was Grace. She held out a large and elaborate bouquet of flowers toward Stella, as if in a gesture of peace. Stella, the surprise showing on her face, stood looking at her for a moment, moving aside to let her in.

'Come in Grace. I'll get you a drink while I put the flowers in water. Edward should be down soon.' She noted that Grace looked hesitant, unsure of the welcome.

Stella handed Grace a glass of wine and went to find a vase for the flowers. The long-stemmed roses were poised and perfect. Their tight blooms were of a dark red, almost black. Their perfection somehow menacing. Looking at them she felt a sense of unease. These were not flowers that she would have chosen for herself.

Edward was making his way down the stairs when he heard the doorbell. Reaching the hallway, he could hear voices coming from the kitchen. He recognised his sister's voice, sounding uncharacteristically subdued. He noted that Stella was silent. He made his way to the kitchen, standing in the doorway unnoticed. This brought back an earlier memory, from an earlier life. The memory of his ex-wife Lydia, standing in exactly the same wary stance as Stella was at this moment, uncertain of what might follow. Grace, as always, dominating the stage. Then they both looked toward him. Stella had a look of relief on her face. Grace had a look of triumph on hers. Edward knew the signs. They were the signs of all those patterns that would go on to form the new patterns. He felt a fleeting sense of inevitability. But he pushed this aside. This time he would be here to protect Stella.

'Edward', Grace said, smiling at him, 'I'm so sorry to intrude on you both. I just wanted to apologize to Stella. My behaviour at the lunch we had was unforgivable. It was the shock of hearing about Adam. I'm afraid that I rather overreacted.'

Stella, looking at Edward, noted the tightening of his jaw. It was the mention of Adam's name. Grace appeared unaware of any tension caused. Instead, she moved to the sideboard and poured herself another drink. It was getting late. Stella had little choice but to ask her to join them for dinner. Edward looked dismayed. Grace looked as if it was what she had expected.

Edward said little over the meal. Stella, trying to cover for his silence, asked Grace about her work. Grace was a photographer of some repute. Most of her work was portraits. Stella had seen some of these works. They were stark, the subjects stripped of all façade. It was as if the camera had been placed inside the subject's head, absorbing all thought and emotion and dissecting these. It was not the world that was looking at the subject, but the subject looking out at the world. Stella had seen a few of the photographs in a small gallery in central London. She had seen the portrait of a smiling young boy and had sensed the evil behind that smile. She had seen the portrait of an old soldier, his face lined and his eyes disillusioned, whose life had been spent in the killing of others. All the works that she had seen had been both piercing and disturbing. All held the bleak outlook as those of Edward's paintings. It was as if both brother and sister had been to a place that others had not been, had seen what others had not seen.

'I saw an exhibition of your work, Grace, a couple of weeks ago.' Stella said. 'It was in a gallery in Covent Garden.'

'Did you?' Grace asked, with some surprise. 'And what did you think of it? What did you really think of it?'

'I thought it was impressive. It showed an insight into the human mind. The mind behind the façade we all keep in place. Apart from the obvious artistic and technical ability, I was quite astonished at the psychological depth.'

At this Edward looked up and stared at Stella intently.
'Yes,' he said rather bleakly, 'we Falconers all have tortured minds. It goes with the territory.' And with that he excused himself from the table, returning to his studio to work. He left without a word to Grace.

Stella was left feeling confused and uncomfortable at Edward's words. She felt that she was taking part in a play, where she was the only one who had not been given a script to read from. When she looked up, she saw that Grace was staring at her. There was a smile on her face, a smile that did not quite reach her eyes. In that one instant, in that one split second, Stella realised that she would always have to exercise caution. That she would always have to be on her guard. She knew, with a great certainty, that she was no match for Grace. And she also knew, with a great certainty, that Grace would find a way to weave herself into their lives. This last was something that she later wished she had heeded more.

21

The following weeks were busy for Stella. The fundraising event that she was part of was not far away. There were long days. There were endless meetings. There were agreements and disagreements, between the various charities involved. Her days formed a pattern. Breakfast with Edward and the morning spent in her study. She would spend the rest of the day in meetings, coming home late most evenings. And although she was tired, this was the best time of the day. She would come home to find Edward waiting for her, the dinner prepared, the table set, a glass of wine handed to her. Edward would ask after her work, asking question after question, carefully listening to her answers. The visit from Grace, although not mentioned, sat as a presence between them. In fact, they had not heard from her since that night. But that was soon to change.

On one of the days when there was a long gap between her meetings, Stella had lunch with Patricia. Although they spoke on the telephone several times a week, they had not seen each other for some time. They had arranged to meet at a small Italian restaurant, near where Stella had her next appointment. When Stella arrived, she saw that Patricia was already there, seated at a table, at the far end of the restaurant. She immediately noticed that there was something different about her. She had that air of calm and serenity that one has, after having found something that has long been searched for.

'Alright,' Stella said, sitting down. 'I can see you've got something to tell me.'

'Would you mind if I brought a guest to your event next month?' she asked. 'There's someone I'd like you to meet.'

'And all this', Stella smiled, 'before you've even poured me a drink? It must be serious. Come on Patricia. All the details please.'

Patricia looked at her for a few moments, strangely shy.

'It's someone I've known for some time. He works on one of the sister magazines. There's always been a tentative friendship between us, but I never let it go any further, as he was married at the time. I didn't want to invite any more drama into my life. God knows, there've been plenty of those. His divorce came through a couple of months ago and we've seen quite a lot of each other since. And…….' Patricia trailed off, noticing that Stella was holding her napkin to her mouth, trying to contain her laughter.

'This is no laughing matter', Patricia said, trying to control her own laughter. 'This is serious.'

'I'm not laughing at you', Stella said, smiling. 'I'm laughing at the fact that you've managed to keep so quiet about it. Usually, I get all the details before you've even gone on the first date. Does this man have a name?'

'Alex. Alex Frayling.' Patricia replied. 'He's kind Stella. He's really kind. I used to think that kindness, in a man, was a sign of weakness. But I now realize that it's a sign of strength, of not wanting to have power or control over someone else.'

Stella sat listening quietly.

'We've established some sort of routine. I cook for him. He cooks for me. He's never late and he calls when he says he will. There is a friendship and there is a passion. There are none of those extravagant gestures that I've had in the past. The ones that lead to a complete burn out, after only a few weeks. And you should see my flat! Gone is the chaos. There are fresh flowers and a fully stocked fridge. Now that I've got someone to share my days with, I realize how lonely I've been. Working too late, drinking too much. The past few months have given my life a framework. A framework I've searched for, for a very long time.'

Stella raised her glass.

'Welcome to the world of shopping lists and dinner parties,' she laughed. 'It's been a long time coming.'

'And you Stella?' Patricia asked. 'Apart from the overload of your work, how are things with you?'

Stella hesitated, a cloud seemingly passing over her face. This did not go unnoticed. Patricia looked worried but said nothing.

Stella told her about the evening of Grace's visit. She told her of the constant tension between Grace and Edward. She told her how obvious it was that Edward appeared to want to place a distance between them.

'It's as if', Stella continued, 'they have a knowledge between them. A knowledge that is a terrible burden to Edward. A knowledge that he can no longer bear. He hasn't once mentioned Grace's name since that night.'

'Can't you talk to him Stella? It's obviously troubling you a great deal. Things like this have to be sorted out, otherwise they reach an out of the ordinary proportion.'

'Sadly, that's not possible. There are areas in Edward's life that are closed to me. I can only enter these when I'm invited and not before.'

'Could it be that they just don't get on together?' Patricia asked. 'It's not that uncommon.'

'No. Adam told me once that as children, Grace and Edward were very close. That they were inseparable in a world they created for themselves. There's something between them that I find quite disturbing. There's something that's made me wary of Grace, frightened even.'

Patricia, realising that Stella was serious and not being fanciful, reached out and took her hand.

'Try and put it to the back of your mind for the time being, Stella. The next few weeks are going to be difficult for you. You can deal with all this at a later time.'

Stella looked up and smiled.

'I can't wait to meet the new man in your life. I'll try not to embarrass you by telling him the stories of your past', she said. 'Thanks for always being there, Patricia', she added on a more serious note. 'It's meant a great deal to me.'

Looking at her, Patricia felt a chill. It was as if Stella had wandered into a labyrinth in her mind, where she could not be reached.

22

The day after her lunch with Patricia, Stella stopped at a second-hand bookshop that she knew well. Her last meeting had finished early, and she was looking forward to a quiet evening with Edward. They were both working such long hours, rarely having much time together. But first she wanted to find a present for Patricia, to celebrate what looked like the start of a promising relationship, with the new man in her life. When she entered the bookshop, she went straight to the cookery section. Here she found exactly what she had been looking for. It was a Victorian book of recipes for dinner parties. This made Stella smile, as Patricia had never given a dinner party in her life. There was a section on how to set the table appropriately, for each type of dinner. There was a section on the etiquette of the dinner party and the placing of guests. On each of the left pages of the book there was a complete menu, from the soup to the coffee. The pages on the right were blank. Here you would keep the notes on the guests invited and what was served on that evening. Stella had trouble stopping herself from laughing, as she imagined Patricia looking through the book. She stopped to buy flowers and made her way home.

It was a little after six o'clock when Stella reached the house. As she let herself in, she was surprised to hear voices coming from the sitting room. Edward never had visitors when he was working. She took off her coat, carrying the flowers to put into water. When she got to the sitting room, she saw Edward and Grace deep in conversation. They had not heard her coming in. They both looked up as she came in, their eyes startlingly alike. Something she had not noticed before.

'Stella', Edward said, getting up. 'I hadn't expected you for another couple of hours. Come and sit down. I'll get us drinks.' He took the flowers from her, kissing the top of her head as he went to the kitchen.

'I dropped by to thank you for the dinner the other night', Grace said. 'And to also ask you more about your fundraising event. I believe that all the charities involved are children's charities.'

'Yes, they are', Stella replied, slightly confused. 'What exactly do you want to know?'

At this moment Edward came in, carrying a bottle of wine and three glasses.

'Grace wants to donate two photographs from her new exhibition, for the auction that you hold. I've put them on the dining room table for you to look at.'

The astonishment showed on Stella's face.

'Are you sure Grace?' she asked. 'That's incredibly generous of you. I really don't know what to say.'

'Wait until you see them first', Grace smiled. 'You might not like them.'

Stella, leaving her glass of wine untouched, went straight to the dining room. She looked first at one photograph and then the other. They were beautiful. The first was a scene set in an orchard. There were several children, the oldest one holding up a younger child to shake the branches of the apple tree. The other children were picking up the fruit and putting them into baskets. The second photograph was that of a young mother holding a baby in the crook of her left arm, smiling down at her other child, whose hand she was holding. In both of the works you could see the poverty of the subjects' lives. But you could also see the serenity. You could see the hope. Stella was deeply moved. She looked at them for a few more moments before she went back to the others.

'Thank you so much Grace', she said, going over and kissing Grace's cheek. 'Thank you so much.'

'You see Stella', Grace said, reading Stella's thoughts, 'I do see beauty and hope in the world. Just not that often.'

Stella remained silent. She looked intently at Grace and wondered about the complexity of the mind behind the façade. She wondered whether she would ever find a way to understand her.

'Anyway', Grace said, 'I'm going to take you both out to dinner. I thought we might go to the French bistro down the road, if that's alright with you both.'

Edward looked questioningly at Stella. Stella, looking forward to a quiet evening with Edward, felt dismayed, but was left with little choice. She could not overlook Grace's generosity. This was something that Grace was more than aware of.

The evening went surprisingly well, with no apparent tension between Grace and Edward. It was still quite early when Stella and Edward returned to the house, Edward going into the kitchen to make coffee and Stella going into the dining room to look at the photographs again. She could not get over the beauty of them, the depth of understanding. She felt that she herself was part of each scene. She felt that could smell the air, that she could taste the fruit. She could feel the softness of the baby in the woman's arms. When she went back into the sitting room, she saw that Edward had put out a tray with the coffee and two glasses of brandy.

'Let's sit out in the garden', he said. 'It's still quite warm.'

Stella followed him out, taking in the scent of the jasmine and the roses. This was their private world, their place of retreat. They sat in silence for a long time; each wrapped in their own thoughts. It was Edward who spoke first.

'I'm sorry about tonight, Stella. I realized when you came in that you were looking forward to a quiet night. So was I. Grace has a way of taking over. She always has had. I know that her donation to your auction was generous, but she rarely does anything without a strong motive. I've no doubt that there'll be some sort of pay back expected. There always is. Just be careful she doesn't draw you into her world.'

'I'm not unaware of all this Edward', she said quietly. 'I've been wary of her from the start. But tonight, couldn't be helped. We'll just have to try and establish some sort of distance, without having it escalate into a confrontation.'

Edward reached over and taking her hand, pressed his lips to her palm.

'Can you play truant one day this week? Come home mid-afternoon? We can lock the door, close the shutters and leave the telephone unanswered. We can watch television and have one of our long dinners at the kitchen table. What do you think?' he asked, a smile in his voice.

'I suppose it's my turn to cook?' Stella replied, grinning.

'That it is my darling. That it is.' Edward moved over to sit by her side, putting an arm around her, folding her close into him.

Stella marvelled at what life had laid at her door. She would take the memory of tonight and folding it quite carefully, would put it away with all the other memories that she treasured. She would keep them for the days when her world was clouded, for the days that she would need the reassurance of the past. She thought all this not realising that that day would come sooner, rather than later. She did not realise that all the folded-up memories she had so carefully stored, would at that time provide her with little comfort, that those memories would provide her with little warmth.

23

Instead of trying to come home early on an afternoon, she took a whole day to herself. She and Edward spent the entire weekend, not unlike excited children, planning the day. They made lists of the things that they wanted to do, of the places they wanted to go to, of the things they would like to eat. As the weekend progressed, these lists got longer. Finally, they gave up, going back to what they always did. They would walk through the park and into Chinatown, going to a small family run Chinese restaurant for lunch. They would make their way home through the side streets, stopping to look through the shops and buying the food for their evening meal. Stella could not help but be conscious of the fact that this was exactly what she would have done if she had been with Adam. Indeed, it was what they had done for the time that she had been with him. We are all creatures of habit and that is why it is so difficult to put the past to one side, for any length of time. The written word, the note of music, the scent of a season, all these enough to open the door to what has gone on before.

When Stella awoke, on that Wednesday morning, her first thoughts were of her day ahead with Edward. She had heard him get up earlier, but she had gone back to sleep. She put on her robe and went downstairs to prepare breakfast. She saw that Edward was already in the kitchen making the coffee. He turned around and folded her into his arms, holding her close for some moments.

'We'll leave as soon as you're ready', he said. 'Let's get out before the telephone starts ringing and you start to find things that you need to do.'

'I have to wait until Frieda gets here', Stella said. 'I have a list of things that need to be done. It won't take long.'

Frieda, the housekeeper, arrived a little before nine o'clock. Stella went through the list she had prepared for her, leaving instructions about the laundry and a delivery she was expecting. Edward, already wearing his coat, was waiting impatiently.

'Sorry to rush you Frieda', he explained. 'We're having a day to ourselves and I'm trying to get Stella out of the house, before she starts thinking of other things to do.'

'Off you go children', Frieda said, smiling. 'Off you go.'

Edward took his mobile telephone out of his pocket and placed it on the sideboard.

'You too Stella', he said. 'Leave your phone as well.'

With that they left the house, one holding the hand of the other.

The day was dull but dry, the light breeze making it good walking weather. They walked up the side streets, stopping occasionally to look into one or another of the shops. The walk across the park took them to the centre of town. Here they stopped for a drink at a bar that was an old haunt of Edward's, before going into Chinatown. When they had reached the restaurant and had ordered their food, they both fell silent, each lost in their thoughts. When Edward spoke it was to mirror the thoughts that had been going through Stella's mind.

'This was what I did with Adam', he said. 'Stopping at the bar we've just been to and then coming on here. It seems like a lifetime ago. Do you ever hear from him, Stella?'

'No', she said. 'No.'

'I really miss him', Edward continued. 'I feel as if a part of my life is missing. I do realize that this has been an awful time for him. I also realize that I'm being selfish, but I'm finding it so difficult. We've had such long years together.'

'We have to give him more time. We have to wait until he's ready', Stella said, reaching out and putting her hand over Edward's. 'He will get in touch. I know he will.'

The Unreal Dance

After lunch they started on their walk home. The walk was largely a silent one. Adam's presence, though invisible, was between them. This was the way it had been from when first they met. Both Stella and Edward had tried hard not to bring Adam into conversation, but he occupied both of their thoughts. It had not been easy.

'We could go to the cinema Stella' Edward said, breaking the silence. 'Or we could go home and have a long and quiet evening.'

'The last sounds rather appealing', she replied. 'We'll close the shutters, lock the door and turn off the telephone.'

'If you're thinking of Grace', Edward laughed, 'she'll always find a way of getting in if she's determined enough.'

But Stella was not thinking of Grace. It was the outside world she was suddenly fearful of. She just wanted to keep it at bay for a few hours longer. It was as if she was afraid of some harm but coming from, she knew not where.

They stopped on the way home to shop for the evening meal, reaching home a little after five o'clock. They were both tired after their walk, their earlier excitement of a day to themselves now somehow muted.

Stella unpacked the shopping and Edward made up the fire in the sitting room. Although still quite mild during the day, there was the start of a chill in the evenings. They had decided on a picnic meal, watching a film on the television. It was much later that Stella checked for messages on her mobile telephone. She was startled to find that there was a text message from Adam. She felt that somehow both she and Edward had conjured him up. The message was brief. "I'm in London for a few days. I'd like to meet, if you have time. We need to talk."

Stella, going back into the sitting room, watched Edward stoking the fire. She decided not to say anything. She would tell him the next day. She did not want to spoil what was left of their evening. This was something that she would soon bitterly regret. It was to lead to a time of distrust between her and Edward. A time of distrust that could have been avoided had she spoken that night. Looking back, she noted the fragility of relationships, the fragility of love.

24

As soon as Stella had left the house the next morning, she telephoned Adam. His voice, although not warm, did not have the abruptness of before. They arranged to meet that evening after Stella had finished her last meeting. The bar where they had arranged to meet was a short walk away from his office. It was where they had met often, when they were living together. The familiarity of the place bringing back memories that she had long stored away.

Stella, arriving a little late, saw Adam as soon as she entered the basement bar. He was sitting at a small table toward the back. It was the table they had always sat at. Looking up he saw her and got up. Although his lips were unsmiling, his eyes held a hunger that he could not hide. There was a bottle of white wine in an ice bucket beside the table. He poured her a glass when she had sat down. He made no move to touch her.

'It's good to see you Adam', Stella said quietly. 'It's been a long while.'

Adam did not reply. He sat staring into his glass, as if he would be able to find the right words in the depths of the wine. When he finally spoke it was in a voice that was almost a whisper, Stella having to lean forward to hear what he was saying.

'I'm at a loss as to what to do Stella. It's an impossible situation. I still don't understand how all this happened. It's been months and yet it feels so immediate. I thought that if I saw you, I would realize that it was all in the past and that I could get on with my life. But I can see that there's little chance of that', he said ruefully. 'I see that it's still too soon.'

'I'm sorry Adam. I really am. You don't have to see me until you're ready, but please see Edward. He's quite lost without you. You've had so much together.'

'You look tired', he said, leaning over to push back a strand of her hair.

'You know how it is. The fundraising event is in less than two weeks. You know how nervous I always get.'

Adam nodded. He did remember. He remembered the restless nights, his trying to soothe her as one would a child, her anxiety almost palpable.

'That's really what I wanted to talk to you about', he said. 'I don't know whether you remember, but you invited my parents to your event when we were with them last. You've obviously forgotten to take them off the guest list, as they received their invitation last week. They insist on coming, having rather taken to you. I hope that's alright.'

'Of course, it is', Stella said. 'Will you be there?'
'No. I think you'll have enough dramas on your hands without me adding to them.'

Stella looked relieved. There were only so many surprises that she could take. It was then that she became aware of someone standing beside her chair. When she looked up, she found her eyes looking up into those of Grace's. She realized how her meeting with Adam must look. She felt as if she had been dealt a body blow. She knew with a certainty of what was to come.

Grace, sitting at a nearby table having a drink with a girlfriend, had been watching them closely for some time. She had noted an intimacy in their conversation.

'Stella, Adam', she said. 'Is Edward with you?'

'No.' Adam replied. 'There are some things of Stella's still at my flat. We were just arranging when they could be moved.'

Stella was grateful for this lie.

'Well', said Grace, looking at the bottle of wine, nestling in the now melting ice cubes, 'it's certainly a very civilized way of sorting things out.

Most people would have just done it with a telephone call.' With that she returned to her table.

Stella's face had paled, her hands clenched in her lap. Adam, knowing Grace well, knew exactly how this would be played out. He was also not unaware of the extent of Edward's anger, of his jealousy. But it was too late to do anything. It was far too late.

'I think I'd like to leave now Adam', she said, looking visibly distressed.

Adam helped her on with her coat. The bottle of wine was left almost full, the two glasses left almost untouched.

'Call me Stella,' he said, with some concern. 'Call me if you need anything.'

When Stella got home, she found Edward in the sitting room. He was sitting staring into a large tumbler of whiskey, the decanter beside him. He did not look up when she came in. The silence was dense. She realized that Grace had already telephoned him. She was not surprised. She had expected this.

Stella took off her coat and went into the kitchen. She needed time to think. Here she saw that the table had been set, and the candles had been lit. There were bowls of vegetables and herbs, prepared and ready to be cooked. Edward had obviously been getting ready the dinner when Grace had telephoned. She went back into the sitting room, taking a chair opposite him.

'I'm sorry I'm late Edward', 'I met Adam for a drink after my meeting.'

'So, I gather,' he said, finally looking up. 'So, I gather.'

'He left me a message yesterday saying that he'd like to meet. He said that he wanted to talk. I thought that I might be able to find a way through this situation. It's been so difficult for all of us.'

'And how often have you met him, to sort out this "situation"? Edward asked, a coldness and a sarcasm in his voice.

'This was the first time, 'Stella said quietly. 'I haven't been hiding anything from you. Why on earth would I?'

Edward was silent for a few moments. He then got up and draining the last of his whiskey, he moved toward the kitchen.

'Come,' he said to Stella, with an unnerving calm, 'I was just finishing preparing the dinner.'

Stella felt uneasy. She remembered the last time she had Edward seen like this. It was the time that they were staying in Lucien's house in Dorset. It was the time that Adam had returned the picture she had given him. That time Edward had waited some days before bringing up the subject. He had bided his time. He had waited for a time when her guard was down, before showing the extent of his anger. Stella knew that this time would be no different. That at some point his rage would not be contained.

The meal was eaten in near silence, Adam's name not mentioned. When they had finished Edward said that he was going up to his studio. He would be working late and that he would sleep in the spare room, so as not to wake her. He had not done that before, always coming to their bed no matter how late the hour. Stella watched him pour himself another large tumbler of whiskey, before he climbed the stairs. She felt a loneliness wrap itself around her. A loneliness that would stay in her memory for a very long time.

It was early when Stella left for work the next morning. She did not see Edward. She had had a sleepless night and was tired before the day had even begun. She was hoping, against hope, that she would remain focused in her work. The time that led up to these charity events was always a difficult one.

Stella's day was not an easy one. She was both tired and apprehensive when she returned home. She was surprised to find Edward in the sitting room looking calm and relaxed. He had laid out a tray with a bottle of wine and two glasses. There was a bowl of plump green olives and a bowl of dark salted almonds.

'Come and sit-down Stella' he said, smiling up at her. 'You look tired. I thought we might go out to eat.'

'I'd love to', Stella said, a degree of wariness in her voice. She was unprepared for this.

They had a quiet dinner at a nearby restaurant, returning home early. Edward slipped her coat off, taking her by the hand and leading her toward the staircase.

'I have a surprise for you', he said, taking her to his studio at the top of the house.

When they reached the studio, Stella saw that Edward had cleared a space on one of the end walls. Here there were three small paintings, one beside the other. They were paintings of a group of children walking forward in a line toward an unknown horizon. In the first painting the figures were faint, their heads bowed down, the horizon bleak. In the second painting the figures were more outlined, their heads becoming raised in some determination, the beginnings of a light on the horizon. The third painting showed the children still in a line, each holding the other's hand, walking with a hope toward the brightly lit sky of dawn. The beauty and the message of these works deeply moved Stella. Again, she was seeing another side to Edward.

Edward watched Stella closely, noting her reaction.

'These are for you Stella', he said, drawing her close. 'They're for the auction.'

'Edward', she said, almost lost for words, 'they're beautiful. They'll fetch a small fortune.'

'I hope so', he said, smiling, 'or I'll know I've lost my touch.'

Stella took another moment to look at them before they went down to bed.

Edward's lovemaking that night had a quietness and a gentleness. Afterward Stella curled into his side before falling asleep. It was some time later that she found herself being pulled abruptly into a sitting position. Edward was holding her tightly, a hand on each of her shoulders. She was still half asleep and only just able to make out his outline in the dark. Yet she could clearly feel the depth of his anger.

'I don't want you to see Adam again without telling me first. I won't put up with this deception. Do you understand me, Stella? Do you understand?'

'I understand', she said, turning away from him. 'I understand.'

She did not say that it was their deception in the first place that had brought them to this. In the morning, she noticed bruise marks on her shoulders, where Edward had gripped her. The marks of fingers digging into flesh, the marks of uncontrolled rage. This episode was never mentioned. Not by either of them.

25

On the day of the charity event Patricia came to the house to collect Stella. This was something she always did before these parties. Stella was grateful for the support. Frieda showed her into the kitchen where Edward and Stella were sitting down, drinking coffee. Edward got up and greeted her warmly.

'You're to look after her Patricia', he said, gesturing toward Stella. 'Make sure she stays off the gin.'

'It's nine o'clock now', Patricia said, smiling at Edward. 'I'll make sure she doesn't have a drop before ten thirty.'

When Stella was ready to leave Edward went to her and held her tightly.

'I'll see you when you come back to change. If you need anything let me know.' He kissed her before letting her go.

When Stella and Patricia arrived at the venue for the party there were dozens of people already there. The high-topped tents had been set up the day before. The tables and chairs were in place. The bar was being set up. There was a secured area housing all the donations for the auction, this being guarded by two security men. Everything appeared to be going according to plan. Stella spent the next few hours with the other members of the charity organisations, seeing to the final details. A little after two o'clock she and Patricia returned to the house to have lunch and to change for the evening. Edward was not there. He had left Stella a note to say that he was having lunch with Lucien and that he would see her later.

Over lunch she told Patricia about her meeting with Adam. She told her how they had run into Grace at the same bar and about the awkwardness that followed. She told her how Grace had been quick to let Edward know. She did not tell her the details of what had later occurred. These were things that she would never speak of to anyone. These were things that would have to remain hidden in a dark corner of her mind, to be remembered at another time.

Patricia stayed silent. She felt deeply uneasy but there was little she could say. The lunch finished, she looked at her watch. They would have to change and leave soon.

They left an hour later arriving at the venue a short time before the event was due to start. The place looked magnificent. The high tents decked in ribbons, the tables set with flowers, the glasses behind the bar gleaming. Stella spoke briefly to one or two of the organizers and then went to find Patricia. When she saw her, she broke into a wide smile. Patricia was standing close to a man whose hand was around her waist. Stella realised that this was Alex, the new man in Patricia's life. She went over to them. Patricia, looking uncharacteristically shy, introduced them.

Alex stepped forward and took Stella by the hand.

'You must be Stella', he said, smiling.

'And you must be the man who's reformed my friend', Stella said, laughing. 'She tells me that she's at last tidied up her flat.'

'That was only because she was looking for my telephone number. I gave it to her months ago. The only way she could find it was to sort out her papers!'

Stella put a hand on his arm and starting to move away, said that she would join them later. It was six o'clock and the start of the evening. The place was almost full. She looked toward the stage where the band was warming up. A few minutes later, Rupert de Vere, who headed all the charities, stepped onto the stage holding a microphone.

'Ladies and gentlemen', he said, 'thank you all for coming here tonight. There are few worthier causes than the plight of children who are disadvantaged, disabled and troubled. With your help we can go some way toward giving them the start in life that they deserve. Enjoy yourselves tonight and please give generously. Thank you again.'

As soon as he had stepped down, the band struck up, the lead singer taking the centre stage. He started with an old Willie Nelson song, "If you've got the money honey, I've got the time."

The crowd started laughing and clapping. The party had begun.

Stella turned to find Edward standing beside her. He took her hand and brushed it with his lips.

'Good choice of song Stella', he said. 'Yours I presume.'

Stella looking past him saw Megan and Brendon, Adam's parents. They had come after all. She felt apprehensive. Edward following her gaze suggested they go over to talk to them. After all, he had known them all his life. Something that Stella had forgotten.

When they reached Adam's parents, there was no awkwardness. Megan stepped forward and kissed Stella's cheek and Brendon gave her a warm hug. They were equally warm in their greeting with Edward.

'Stella my dear', Megan said, 'this all rather splendid. You must have all worked very hard.' She placed her hand on Stella's arm and took her to one side.

'Brendon and I would like to make a donation', she said, handing Stella an envelope. 'We won't be staying long. We're having dinner with Adam. He thought it best not to come.'

Stella said that she understood, and she thanked them for coming. She noted a rather wistful look in Megan's eyes. A look that said she wished that things could have turned out differently. It was now that Stella saw Grace standing a few feet away. She went over to her. Unusually, Grace looked a little unsure of herself, not knowing what to expect of Stella.

'Thank you for coming Grace,' she said, a coldness in her voice. 'And thank you again for the generous donation. The auction will be held toward the end of the evening. I do hope you can stay.'

'I'm sorry about the other night Stella', she said, in a subdued voice. 'It's just that I've always been rather protective of Edward.'

'Edward doesn't need protecting', Stella replied. 'I would have told him as soon as I'd got home. This has been a difficult time for all of us. But you managed to make it worse.' Stella walked away, remembering Edward's anger the previous week. Edward, who had heard this conversation, said nothing but made sure to stay by Stella's side for the rest of the evening.

The high note of the evening was the auction. There were two professional auctioneers and a compere. The amount of the money that was reached was beyond all expectation, with Edward's paintings going for a sum that even he could not believe.

'Well', Stella said, taking Edward's hand and squeezing firmly, 'maybe this is how we should sell your paintings. And can you imagine the percentage I could take?'

'I can', he said, laughing. 'But I'll leave it up to you to break it to my agent. I'm far too afraid of her.'

When the evening ended Stella took Edward to where Patricia and Alex were sitting. Edward kissed Patricia and shook Alex's hand.

'You're a brave man Alex', he said. 'You're not taking on one woman, but two. These two are inseparable.'

'I'm beginning to realise that', Alex said, laughing. 'I shall count on you for support.' With that he took Patricia's arm, and they left.

Edward turned to Stella, brushing her hair back with his hand.

'Let's go home', he said. 'You look tired. And anyway, there's something that I want to talk to you about.'

When they got home Edward sat Stella down and went to the sideboard to pour them each a large brandy. He handed Stella her glass and sat down opposite her.

'How long will it take', he asked her, 'to tie up all the ends after tonight?'

'Not long', she replied. 'Most of it is out of my hands now. It shouldn't take more than two or three days. Why do you ask?'

'You know that I was having lunch with Lucien today. Well, he suggested that we might like to use his house in Dorset, sometime in the next few weeks. After that he'll be staying there himself. He always does that when he's finishing writing a book. With my exhibition coming up in the New Year I'll be working long hours. It would be good to spend some time alone together before that.'

'God Edward, that would be wonderful', Stella said, excitement in her voice. 'It would be really wonderful.'

'We can go for a whole week. And when we get back it'll be your turn to look after me. I'll expect lavish meals every night and beautifully pressed shirts every day.'

'Understood', Stella said, laughing.

It was some weeks later that Stella would come to the realisation that this was the week that would, dramatically, change both their lives. This would be the point of no return for both of them.

26

The week that Stella and Edward spent in Dorset was a time that would be remembered. A time that they would both look back on with memories that they would hold dear. It was a time of calm and understanding. It was to be the stepping stone that would usher in a new chapter in their lives.

They established a routine. Each day they would take a long walk along the beach. They would then go to the nearby village to shop for food, ending up at the local pub where they would have lunch. The afternoons were spent in the first floor sitting room, which looked out toward the sea. Later Edward would make up a fire in the large stone fireplace, while Stella prepared the evening meal. After eating they sat on the veranda outside the sitting room, each wrapped in a blanket as the nights had turned quite chill. Here they would sit and talk for long hours, only going in to sit by the fire when the air got too cold.

It was on the third night that Edward first spoke of Adam. Stella had been so far careful to not mention his name.

'I apologise for reacting so badly to you meeting with Adam', he said. 'I was both jealous of you seeing him and not telling me first and I was jealous of the fact that he hadn't contacted me. I can't tell you how much I miss him. I can't stop thinking about it.'

'We'll get there Edward. We will get there. But nothing can be done until he's ready. His loss has been greater than ours. It's going to take time.'

Edward leant over and touched her cheek.

'And I'm sorry about Grace', he continued. 'She had no right to interfere, but it's what she does best. I understand why you did what you did, and I know that you would have told me. It's just that when Grace telephoned, I felt such a great anger. I'd already lost Adam, and I was afraid of losing you too.'

'You haven't lost Adam', Stella said, taking his hand. 'And you'll never lose me.'

'You're a homemaker Stella. It was only that night, waiting for you to come back, that I realised how empty the house had been without you. It's the same with Adam. His work is a lonely one. All the traveling. all the hotels. You took the sting out of that. You gave him something to look forward to. You were building a future together. Now that future's been taken away. He's been left in a wilderness.'

Edward's words had deeply saddened Stella. Yet he was only voicing what had been on her mind for the past months.

'Come', she said to him, 'let's go in. It's suddenly become unbearably cold out here.'

Over the next few days Stella noticed a great change in Edward. It was as if he had laid down a heavy burden. He had placed all his thoughts and all his fears in a space between them. The weight of these could be shared by both of them. They had proved too heavy for him alone. He started to talk to Stella about Adam. About their time at school, about the years that followed. It seemed that even in his absence, Adam was back with them, that he was back in their lives.

'I'm going to telephone him when we return', Edward said over lunch one day. 'I don't care if he doesn't want to talk to me. I'll carry on until he does.'

Stella remained silent.

'And I don't mind if you see him, Stella. I really don't. I can see that if anyone can sort this mess out it'll be you.'

'We'll do it together', she said, smiling. 'That way he won't be able to put up much of a fight.'

The Unreal Dance

Their remaining few days proved to be the happiest ones that Stella could remember. Gone was the tension. Gone were the unanswered questions. The weather had turned, bringing with it a heavy rain and a sharp wind. They spent their time in front of the fire, Stella reading and Edward drawing. On the last evening while Stella was sitting in front of the fire, Edward left the room for a few moments and returned, carrying a small velvet pouch. He placed this in Stella's lap. Edward watched her as she opened the pouch. He saw the surprise on her face. It was a small gold box inlaid with a square cut emerald. The box was heavy with gold, the green of the emerald clear and mesmerizing.

'It's to keep your memories in Stella,' Edward said, watching her face. 'But only the good ones.'

'If I'm to keep my good memories in a box Edward, you're going to have to get me a much larger one. This one is barely big enough to hold those of the few days.'

'I see that you're going to turn out to be an expensive woman', he laughed. 'A very expensive woman.'

Stella went over to sit beside him, resting her head on his chest.

'Thank you', she said, reaching up to kiss him. 'It's beautiful. I wish I had got something to give you.'

'You've given me enough Stella. You've given me more than enough.'

27

When Stella and Edward returned home the following day, Frieda was still there. The house was filled with the scent of flowers and of wood polish. The kitchen was filled with the warm smell of cooking. The fire in the sitting room had been lit.

'My God Frieda', Stella said, going over to kiss her cheek, 'what a welcome.'

'I thought this morning when I saw what the weather was like', Frieda said, gesturing toward the heavy rain outside, 'that you wouldn't want to come back to a cold house. I've made a casserole that I've left in the oven. It's beef and dumplings cooked in red wine.'

'I'm blessed', Edward said, giving Frieda a hug, 'I'm really blessed. Now I've got two women to spoil me.'

Frieda looked at Edward intently. She had worked for him for a great many years. She had never before seen him so relaxed or so happy. She smiled to herself as she went into the kitchen to make tea.

Over dinner that night Edward brought up the subject of Lucien.

'I'd like to invite him over to dinner in the next couple of weeks. I sent him a dozen bottles of his favourite wine the last time we stayed at his house, but I'd really like you to meet him. We could invite Patricia and Alex at the same time. What do you think?'

'A dinner party Edward?' Stella said, jokingly. 'Won't that be bad for your image?'

'I must say it'll be a first', he said. 'We'll just have to keep very quiet about it. Swear the others to secrecy. The image of the brooding and reclusive artist is one I've carefully cultivated over the years. I mustn't disappoint my public.'

After dinner Edward telephoned Lucien. Lucien said he would be free any night that suited them. Stella telephoned Patricia and the dinner was arranged for the following week. As Edward had said, this was a first. Since Stella had moved in, they rarely had anyone to the house. It had just been the two of them.

It was early when Edward went up to his studio the next morning. Stella worked in her study for a few hours and left the house without disturbing him. She left him a note to say that she would be back in the late afternoon. And that he was to call her if he wanted anything. She had made up her mind what she was going to do. She was going to try and contact Adam. She was determined to try and sort things out between him and Edward. It was time. It was more than time.

Stella bought a newspaper and went to a nearby café. She ordered a coffee and sat down staring out onto the street. Her coffee went cold, and the newspaper remained unopened. Finally, she picked up her telephone and called Adam. He showed no surprise at hearing from her, as if he had been waiting for her call.

'Can we meet Adam?' she asked him, hesitantly. 'I'd like to talk to you. We never really got the chance when we last met.'

'I'm going back to Washington the day after tomorrow. Can we meet in an hour's time?'

'That would be fine', she said. 'Where shall I see you?'

At this Adam hesitated as if trying to make up his mind about something.

'Can you come around to the flat?' he asked. 'I'm in the middle of packing.'

Stella said that she would. When she arrived an hour later, she stood on the front steps for a few moments before ringing the doorbell. She had lived here for a year but felt that somehow, she was visiting the house of a stranger. There was no sense of familiarity about it. She pressed the doorbell, apprehensive of what was to come.

Adam, after receiving Stella's telephone call, had spent the last hour pacing the floor. He had left his clothes unpacked and his work untouched. He was having doubts about meeting Stella. The last time they met he had been overcome by an overwhelming longing for her, an overwhelming longing for the life that they had shared together. He was surprised to find that even after all the time that had gone by, his feelings for her had not changed.

Adam opened the door and taking Stella's coat, showed her into the sitting room. He watched her face as she stood there looking around, as she tried to imagine herself as she had lived within these walls, as she tried hard to gather the memories. But he could see that she remembered little. He could see that she did not remember the meals that they had shared together, the long talks that they had in the evenings and all the plans that they had made for their future.

'Sit down Stella', he said, finally. "I'll get you a glass of wine and you can tell me what it is that you want to talk about. At least this time we won't get interrupted.'

When he returned with her drink, she noted that he did not have one for himself. It was then that she saw the tumbler of whiskey on the table. It was unlike Adam to drink spirits during the day. He sat down opposite her and looked at her questioningly.

'Adam', she said so quietly, that he had to lean forward to hear her speak, 'we need to sort this situation out.'
'What situation Stella? Do you mean the situation that you and Edward brought about?' There was bitterness in his voice.

'It's not so much for me as for Edward. I was the one at fault and for that I'm deeply sorry.' Stella sat back in the chair and looked at him with an intensity that he found disturbing. 'Don't wipe out all the years that you shared with Edward, Adam', she continued, 'It's like wasting a whole lifetime. You're throwing away a friendship that's rare between two people.'

Adam looked at her with absolute astonishment.

The Unreal Dance

'Are you serious Stella? Are you really serious? Have you both suddenly re-written the rules on friendship?' He took a large sip from his whiskey, staring down into the tumbler as if looking for the answers to his questions.

'Edward's going to call you, Adam', Stella said wearily. 'And he's going to go on calling you. He's not going to give up. It's up to you where the two of you go from there. I just hope that you remember what the two of you had.' With that Stella got up, saying that she had to leave. She noted the look of loneliness and of utter hopelessness on Adam's face when she left.

When Stella returned home, she found a note from Edward to say that he had gone to collect some paints. She was glad. She did not want him to see the misery that was apparent on her face. She tried to distract herself by looking through the various cookery books that she had. She would need to start planning for the dinner party the following week. She wanted it to go well. It was a very long time since she had done something like this. When she had lived with Jack, no one had ever come to the house. He did not seem to have any friends outside of the office. And any spare time that he had was spent with the other women, whose beds he had shared. With Adam there had been little time with his work and his traveling. They had wanted to spend any time that they had together. With Edward it looked as if they were about to join the normality of the outside world. This last gave Stella a feeling of warmth, a feeling of permanence.

When Edward returned, he saw Stella sitting in front of a pile of cookery books, making notes. He pulled her to her feet, laughing.

'Are we going to be like other people Stella?' he asked, voicing the thoughts that she had had earlier. "Are we going to be a normal couple?' He seemed to be happy at the thought when he said all this.

"We'll try; she joked. 'We'll really try.'

Stella did not tell him that she had been to see Adam. She did not want to spoil this moment.

28

On the day of the dinner party Stella arose early. Although she had planned everything some days before, she wanted to make sure that nothing was left to chance. The lamb shanks in red wine and rosemary had been slowly cooked the day before and left overnight to absorb its juices. The poached pears in white wine, honey and cinnamon would be prepared that afternoon. The roasted vine tomatoes on garlic brioche would be done just before the meal. Edward had taken charge of the wine, choosing a different one for each course. He had said jokingly that it was a job for the head of the household.

When Frieda arrived, she could see how excited Stella was. She was excited too. In all the years that she had worked for Edward, she had never known him have guests for dinner. This house had finally become a home she thought.

That evening Lucien arrived early. Edward introduced Stella to him.

'Lucien', he said, 'this is Stella. The love of my life.'

'I can see that', Lucien said, laughing and noting the flowers and the lit candles. You're a reformed character. I'm delighted to meet you Stella', he continued. 'I've never seen this side of Edward before. It shows that there's hope for all of us.'

'It hasn't been easy', Stella said smiling, 'it's actually been quite hard work. But I'm slowly getting there.' She returned to the kitchen leaving them to talk. She checked that everything was ready and went back into the sitting room to join them. Patricia and Alex arrived a short while later. After the introductions Edward served drinks. It was nine o'clock before they sat down to eat. She looked up and saw Edward smiling at her. She smiled back.

The dinner was going well, everyone at ease. There was a great deal of laughter as Edward recounted stories about his agent. About how difficult she was, about how she never stopped nagging him.

'You know', he said, 'when she first started representing me, she wore nothing but jeans and oversized jumpers. Now she wears Chanel suits and carries Hermes handbags. I can't help but feel that there's something wrong there.'

'Not at all', Lucien said, laughing. 'She's just trying to show the world how well you're doing.'

'I suppose that that's one way of looking at it', Edward said, philosophically. 'But look at Stella and myself. We're dressed in rags.'

It was while everyone was laughing at this that the doorbell rang. It was after eleven o'clock. Stella immediately stiffened. She knew who it was. And so did Edward. He looked at her with a resigned expression on his face and went to open the door.

'I was just passing', Grace could be heard saying, 'and I saw that all your lights were on.'

'It's after eleven o'clock', Edward said, wondering how she could just be passing. She lived on the other side of London.

Grace walked past him, only stopping when she saw the others sitting around the table. The astonishment showed on her face. It was as if she had walked into someone else's house by mistake. The table had gone quiet. Edward introduced his sister.

'My God Edward', Grace said, 'things have really changed around here. You've changed. None of this', she said, gesturing toward the room, 'is you.'

'It is now', he said coldly. 'It is now.' And wanting to diffuse the situation he asked her to sit down and handed her a glass of wine. He noted that Grace had not even acknowledged Stella's presence. He also saw that this had not gone unnoticed by the others. Stella was sitting very still, visibly shaken. The talk at the table had stopped.

'Grace', said Stella, pulling herself together and getting up from the table, 'there's some dessert left. Come with me to the kitchen. You can carry the cheese in.' Grace, taken aback, followed Stella. When they were in the kitchen Stella closed the door before turning to Grace.

'Don't you ever turn up here unannounced again. I'm getting tired of all your dramas. Where you go trouble follows. I've had enough. I really have. And when we go back to the others, I'd like you to behave as any normal guest would. Otherwise, I'll ask you to leave.' Stella's tone brooked no argument.

When they returned to the dining room Edward noted that Grace was strangely silent. The conversation at the table had become awkward and stilted, no one able to cover up what had gone on before, no one able to fully understand. The evening had gone flat.

When everyone had left Edward sat Stella down, taking her hand in his.

'I'm sorry Stella', he said quietly. 'I'm so very sorry. Grace's behaviour was unforgivable.'

'It doesn't matter Edward', Stella said, quite calmly. 'It won't be happening again. That I can promise you.'

Edward looked at her noticing a new change, a new resolve.

He never asked her about the exchange that had taken place when she and Grace had left to go into the kitchen. And Stella never offered to tell him. All he knew was that they did not see Grace again for some months. And by this time the course of their lives had changed to a greater extent than they could have thought imaginable.

29

It was some weeks later that Stella noticed how tired she was feeling. She was sleeping well but it was as if a fatigue was gripping her body. Then she noticed a tenderness in her breasts and a reaction to the smell of coffee. She did not have to check the date of her last monthly period in her diary. She knew by instinct that she was pregnant. The timing coincided with the time that she and Edward had spent that week in Dorset. She telephoned Patricia.

'Patricia' she asked, 'can you take a few hours off tomorrow?'

'Of course I can', Patricia said. 'Is there anything the matter? Only you sound a little strained.'

'I think I'm pregnant Patricia. In fact, I'm almost certain I am.'

'Have you spoken to Edward about this?'

'No.' Stella said quietly. 'This was not planned. The subject of children has never come up between us. I'm afraid Patricia. I'm really afraid. If he doesn't want the child, then that'll be the end of us.'

'Wait until you're sure Stella. There's no point in worrying about anything until you're absolutely sure. What time do you want me to come tomorrow?'

'Come around noon', Stella said. ''Edward won't be here then. He's having lunch with his agent.'

In the event Stella was right to fear talking to Edward about all this. Even she could not have anticipated the extent of his reaction when she finally told him.

The following day Patricia arrived a little after midday. She was carrying a bottle of wine in one hand and a plastic bag in the other.

'The wine is for me', she said smiling, 'and the bag is for you.'

Stella, taking the bag, looked inside. There were two different brands of pregnancy kits. The first that she used was positive, as was the second that she tried an hour later. But she had never had any doubts as to the outcome. They went into the kitchen to have lunch, neither of them having a great deal to say, both lost in their own thoughts.

'Will you tell Edward tonight?' Patricia asked.

'No', Stella replied quietly. 'He won't be back until late. I'll tell him tomorrow.'

After Patricia had left Stella telephoned Dr. Feingold's surgery and made an appointment for the following afternoon. He would help her sort out her thoughts, which were by now beginning to tumble one over the other. She would tell Edward after that.

When Stella went to the surgery the next day, she noted that it was quite empty. She was the last patient of the day and was shown in immediately.

'Sit down Stella', Dr. Feingold said. 'Sit down. I must say you're looking remarkably well. What can I do for you?'

'I'm pregnant', Stella said shyly, staring down at her hands.
'And you're happy about this?' he asked.

'I am', she smiled at him. 'Very happy.'

'How does Adam feel?'

Stella looked perplexed, suddenly realizing that she had not seen Dr. Feingold since her illness over a year ago.

'I'm no longer with Adam', she said. "We separated some time ago. I'm now with someone called Edward. Edward Falconer.'

'Edward Falconer the artist?' Dr. Feingold asked, with some surprise. 'That Edward Falconer?'

'Yes', Stella replied.

'I have a painting of his from one of his first exhibitions', he said. 'It hangs in my study at home. A complex mind. A very complex mind.' Dr. Feingold, as well as being a medical doctor, was also a noted psychiatrist.

'Well,', he continued, 'how does Edward feel about this pregnancy?'

'I haven't told him about it yet', Stella said quietly. 'The subject of children has never even come up between us.'

'Do it sooner rather than later Stella', he said. 'When a child is not planned, the man must have time to adjust. Fear of fatherhood and fear of the responsibility it entails are not uncommon. It can be quite a frightening prospect.'

He asked Stella exactly how long she thought it was since she had fallen pregnant. She told him that it was between six and seven weeks. She explained that it was during a week that she and Edward had spent away. He briefly examined her and made a few notes before coming around to where she was sitting, holding out his hand.

'Thank you, Dr. Feingold,', Stella said, getting up, 'I'll tell Edward tonight.'

'Please call me if you have any questions or if you need to talk. After all, I've known you since you were a teenager and so there won't be any surprises there', he smiled. 'Come and see me in two weeks' time.'

When Stella arrived back home Edward was out. He had left her a note to say that he would return around seven o'clock and that he was looking forward to a leisurely and lavish dinner. Stella smiled to herself. She had already planned the meal the day before. She had already been rehearsing the words that she would say to him. She put on some music and went into the kitchen. She had made a lemon and thyme chicken casserole that morning. She added a glass of dry white wine to the casserole and placed it in the oven. She cut off the stems from the dark purple sprouting broccoli, arranging them on a plate ready to be steamed. She tossed the new potatoes in olive oil and rosemary sprigs. She set the table with great care. She sat down and waited for Edward.

When Edward returned the house was filled with the warm smell of cooking. He was smiling as he went into the kitchen, knowing that Stella would be in there. He went over to her and pulled her to her feet, kissing her deeply.

'My God, Stella', he said, 'to think that all my life I've shied away from domesticity. And now I'm so blissfully happy. Can I get you a drink?' Stella said no.

Edward poured himself a whiskey and sat down opposite her.

'I've just been to see the gallery for my new exhibition', he told her. 'It's a wonderful space. It has a large area where the sculptures will go and smaller areas to house the paintings. I'm already starting to feel quite excited about it.'

Edward took a sip of his drink and looked intently at Stella. She was unusually quiet.

'Are you alright darling?' he asked her. 'You seem a little preoccupied.'

All the words that Stella had been rehearsing to say to him went out of her head. All the ways of telling him gently seemed to have left her.

'Edward', she said, waiting for his reaction, 'I'm pregnant.'

Stella saw that Edward's face had gone pale and that his jaw had tightened. He put down his glass and looked at her with a bleak look in his eyes.

'Are you sure Stella?' he asked her. 'Are you absolutely sure?'

There was no need for her to reply. Edward could see the answer in her face. He put down his glass and without another word got up and left the house. This was not the reaction that Stella had expected. She remained sitting at the table, staring out of the window. She waited for Edward to return but he did not. She turned off the oven and blew out the candles. A little before midnight she went up to bed. When she finally found sleep, it was a troubled one. She dreamt again of the park where she used to go walking. She saw the two children sailing their model boat on the pond. When she reached them, they turned around. Their faces were like that of Edward's. As she put out her hand to them, they disappeared, leaving no trace. When Stella awoke the next morning, her pillow was wet with her tears.

Edward did not return that day, nor did he return the next or the next. Stella did not telephone him, and he did not telephone her. Her days were spent in a void of bewilderment and misery, all her questions left unanswered.

30

It was the evening of the fourth day when Edward returned home. Stella was in the sitting room. She had made her decision. If Edward did not want this child, she would leave. She still had her flat. It would do for the time being. She felt a tide of sadness wash over her. She had hoped for so much more than this. But she was left with little choice.

Edward, entering the sitting room, went over to Stella. He made no move to touch her, standing beside her silently for some moments. When he finally spoke, his voice was barely audible.

'I'm sorry Stella', he said. 'I'm truly sorry. My behaviour's been unforgivable. I have no excuses, only an explanation. Can we talk? Will you give me the chance to explain?'

Stella put down her teacup and looked up at him. His eyes were dull, his face pale and unshaven. He was wearing a new shirt that had obviously come straight from the packaging, the lines of the folds still quite prominent.

'I can't imagine any explanation justifying the way that you behaved', she said. 'I'd made up my mind to leave. You were right to say that your behaviour was unforgivable. You've put me through days and nights of doubt and misery.'

Edward went to the sideboard and poured himself a large whiskey. He sat down opposite Stella and looked at her for a few moments, before saying anything.

'My reaction was borne out of fear Stella', he said. 'It was borne out of my fear of loss. It has seemed to me that everything that I've ever held dear has been taken away from me.'

Edward stopped and took a sip of his drink.

'There was the death of my sister Lily, the death of the unborn child that Lydia was carrying, the disappearance of Adam from our lives. There was the fact that Grace's presence was like a thread, running through all this. And I appeared to be the source of that thread. All the questions and doubts that I'd so deeply buried surfaced at the same time. I know that it may sound irrational, but I was suddenly afraid for you and our child. I thought that if I wasn't here then no harm would come to either of you.'

Stella sat quietly looking at Edward's troubled face. The changing expressions mirrored the memories that he had for so long buried.

'Before Lily was born, it was just Grace and myself. We were very close. But soon I realized that Grace's love for me was becoming claustrophobic. It was becoming a complicated and oppressive love. It was too much of a responsibility. When Lily was born things changed. Lily's love for me was a joyous one. It was unconditional and uncomplicated. We became inseparable. At first, I didn't notice that Grace was becoming more and more withdrawn. She wouldn't play with Lily; she wouldn't touch her. It was as if the child didn't exist. And I noticed, after a while, that Lily would not go near her. That she didn't want to be left alone with her. That day that Lily died will remain etched on my mind forever. The figure of the drowned child, the figure of the drowned puppy, an orange ball bobbing up and down on the water. To this day I cannot understand why Grace had chosen to look after her. It had not happened before.' Edward's words were becoming quieter and quieter. Stella had to lean forward to hear him. It was as if he was lost in the dense shadows of his past.

'When I married Lydia', he continued, 'I was hoping for a new beginning. But I realized that the marriage was a mistake almost from the start. We came from two completely different worlds and could not manage to find a middle ground between us. Neither of us was happy. If she had not fallen pregnant, we would almost certainly have separated.' Edward took a large sip of his drink before going on.

'Lydia was four months pregnant when she fell down the stairs. She lost the child. Grace had gone to the house to ask her out to lunch. Lydia had gone upstairs to change and, in her haste, had fallen. After the loss of the child, she had a complete mental breakdown. She was in a clinic for several months. I only saw her once after that. She made it quite clear that she wished to put that part of her life behind her.'

Edward looked up, trying to fathom Stella's reaction to all this. It was something that he had never spoken of before. It was something that he had hidden, even from himself. The weight of this burden had been too heavy to bear.

Stella sat staring down at the table. All Edward's questions and doubts and suspicions had been laid before her. Each of these had a form and a weight. It was now up to her as to what importance she would place on them. She had heeded Edward's words. She could now understand why he had reacted in the way that he had.

Stella reached over and took his hand. She could not bear to see the torment that he was going through. She had never been one for recriminations and postmortems.

'You're forgiven', Stella said sternly. 'But there is a condition.'

'Anything', Edward replied simply, 'anything.'

'You've got to take me out for a Chinese meal tonight', Stella smiled, 'I've been dreaming about it for four days.' This was no time for recriminations, she thought, this was no time.

Edward went over to her and folding her into his arms, placed his chin on to the top of her head.

'Thank you, Stella,', he said gently, 'thank you for everything.'

'Edward', Stella said, moving away from him, 'much as I like the comfort of your arms, all I can think about right now is Chinese food. Bowls and bowls of it.'

Edward laughed, releasing her from his hold.

The Unreal Dance

'I can just imagine', he said, 'that the first words that the child utters will be in Mandarin Chinese. And that it'll be sitting in its highchair eating the pureed food with chopsticks.'

'First things first Edward', Stella said, pulling him toward the front door, 'first things first.'

When they returned from the restaurant Edward took Stella by the hand and led her to the kitchen. He sat her down and made her tea. He then told her that he needed to go upstairs but would be down in a few moments. When he came back, he was holding a small box in his hand. He put this on the table between them.

'I was going to wait until after my exhibition', he told her, opening the box. 'But I think that now is the right time. I don't want you to ever have any doubts about how I feel about you. I don't want you to think that my asking you to marry me has anything to do with you being pregnant. I had this ring made soon after I first met you. You had my heart from that very first time.'

Stella took the ring from Edward's outstretched palm. It was of two hands, one holding the other. Each hand was a separate ring, fastened to the other at the base. It was of heavy dull gold. The two hands, when pulled apart, revealed a third ring sitting beneath them. This was a square cut emerald sitting on a plain band. The third ring was not attached to the other two and could be worn on its own. Stella sat staring down at the ring, her eyes misted with tears. When she looked up, she noted the anxiety in Edward's face.

'Well Stella?' he asked. 'Well?'

Stella held out her left hand and gave him the ring to put on her finger. Edward slipped the ring onto her finger and placed a kiss on it.

'This is forever, Stella', he said. 'Promise me that?'

'I promise', she said solemnly. 'I promise.'

Thinking back to her happiness at that moment, Stella realized that they should not have attracted the attention of the jealous Gods. That the happiness that was theirs should have been wrapped in fine cloth and put somewhere, away from their prying eyes.

31

It was after seven o'clock the next morning when Stella awoke. She was surprised to find that Edward was still beside her in the bed. He would usually get up around dawn and go straight up to his studio. He was lying with his eyes closed, one hand resting against her face and the other resting protectively over her stomach. Stella tried to get up without waking him but saw that his eyes were already open. He smiled at her.

'I've been lying here awake for hours', he said. 'I've been imagining the sound of a child's voice ringing around the house. I've been imagining the sound of a child's footsteps on the stairs. I can't wait for the time when I can go down to the local pub in the evenings and stand at the bar with all the other men who have children. I'd buy them all a drink and complain about the baby crying in the night. I'd complain about the chaos in the house and about tripping up over the scattered toys. It'll be a whole new world for me, Stella. A whole new beginning.'

'And you'll complain about my cooking', she laughed, 'and how I've put on weight and let myself go.'

'Of course I will', he said, sitting up, 'all that goes without saying. But first I'm going to make you breakfast. I'm going to take a few days off', he said, leaning over and pushing a strand of Stella's hair away from her face. 'We need to talk and to make plans.'

After Edward had gone down Stella went into the bathroom. She stood in front of the mirror and looked at herself. Her breasts were slightly fuller and her hips almost imperceptibly more rounded. Smiling to herself she put on the embroidered robe that Edward had given her, when she first moved here, tying the belt and going downstairs.

Over breakfast Edward reached out and took Stella's hand in his.

'What do you think of getting married as soon as the arrangements can be made?' he asked her.

'You mean you don't want to walk down the aisle with me when I'm eight months pregnant, wearing a large confection of cream lace and satin and with my swollen feet and puffy ankles peeking out from under my skirts?' she smiled.

'I won't care what you look like, Stella', he replied. 'I'm just thinking of our poor children in the years to come. I'm thinking of their embarrassment when they see their mother in the wedding photographs, barely able to walk, carrying a bouquet of flowers in one hand and duck spring rolls in the other.'

'Well,', said Stella, 'to save you all that embarrassment I think that we should start on the arrangements straight away.'

'I'll call my parents. I know that Grace is staying with them for a few days. We can drive up there tomorrow. We may have to stay overnight if that's alright with you. There are some legal documents I need to go over with my father.
'I'd like that', Stella said. 'I never did get to see the house or the grounds the last time.'

Edward telephoned his parents and arranged that he and Stella would drive up the next day, staying the night and returning the following day. After the conversation he noted that his mother had not even asked him the reason for his sudden visit. The last visit had been some time ago.

The next day they left early, taking the longer route through the small villages that Edward wanted to show Stella. They stopped for tea and bought bread from a local bakery, to take home with them. They arrived at the house just before lunchtime. Mrs. Dawlish was there to greet them.

'You look well, Edward,' Mrs. Dawlish said, patting Edward on the arm. 'And you, Stella. You look positively radiant.' She looked at Stella closely. 'Well,', she said, beaming, 'well.'

Stella realized that although Mrs. Dawlish made no comment, she knew. She smiled back shyly.

'Come,' Mrs. Dawlish said. 'I'm about to serve lunch. The others are in the dining room.'

When they entered the dining room Magnus got up from the table and after shaking Edward's hand, he kissed Stella on the cheek. Angela barely acknowledged them, and Grace raised her head, lifting one hand in a silent greeting. After the food had been served Angela looked up and addressed her son.

'It's good to see you both', she said, 'but I got a sense of urgency from your telephone call, Edward. Is there something wrong?'

'Not at all, Mother', Edward replied. 'Stella and I are getting married. We'd like to go ahead with the wedding as soon as all the arrangements can be made.'

Stella looked around the table. Magnus was smiling, Angela was staring down at her plate and Grace had gone quite pale. There were no words of congratulation.

'I don't understand', Angela said, finally looking up. 'Why are you doing things in such a hurry? You've got a big exhibition coming up. Can't you at least wait until after that?'

'Stella's pregnant, Mother. We're going to have a child. I was going to ask her to marry me after the exhibition anyway. But we've decided that now is a better time for both of us.'

Stella looked up at Edward's mother. Angela's eyes held a bleakness; they held a look of sorrow at memories past. Grace, quite visibly upset, had knocked over her glass, the red of the wine seeping into the white of the tablecloth like that of blood. She made no move to clear it up.

'Well, my dears', Angela said, quickly composing herself, 'we'd better start making the arrangements as soon as possible. You could have the blessing in our family chapel and the reception here.' She was remembering the rather sterile Registry Office, when Edward had married Lydia and the dull reception afterwards, in the local hotel.

The Unreal Dance

Edward, taking Stella's hand under the table, looked to her silently for her answer.

'Thank you, Angela,', Stella said. 'We'd love that.' It was the first time that she had seen Angela smile.

'And Stella,' Angela continued, 'you can have Edward's cot if you like. It's been in the family for years. First Edward had it and then Grace and then…' Here Angela faltered. She had been about to say Lily's name. Her eyes were misted with tears as she looked down at the table. The silence that filled the room was unyielding, a shadow cast. It was as if a ghost had entered and sat down amongst them. Stella looked at Edward, not knowing what to expect. She was astonished at the expression on his face. There was a calm and serenity about him, as if a ghost had finally been laid to rest.

'Thank you, Mother', he said. 'I'll show it to Stella later. I'm sure she'll love it. But you never know with these modern women', he continued jokingly, 'she might want one in plastic.' The mood in the room had lightened. The ghost had, for the time being, left them alone with a semblance of peace.

After lunch Edward and Magnus went into the study. Edward explained to Stella that a great deal of paperwork had to be gone through and that he would come and find her when everything was finished. Grace had already gone up to her room. Angela, taking Stella by the arm, offered to show her around the grounds and the house. Stella was delighted, asking if they could go to the chapel first. It was a short walk from the house, reached through a small, wooded area. When they got to the chapel she felt as if her breath had been taken from her. Shafts of light were coming down through the branches of the tall trees, lighting up the colours of the stained-glass windows. In front of the chapel there was a stone fountain. Behind the chapel there was a small graveyard.

'I've always loved this place', Angela said. 'It was here that I married Magnus. There is both a remoteness and an intimacy about it. I sometimes come here just to sit and think. It gives me a sense of peace.' They both stood there for some moments, each lost in their own thoughts, then made their way back. There now seemed to be a warmth and an understanding between them that had not been there before.

After supper that evening, they all sat by the fire in the drawing room. Edward and his father talked about the estate and Angela and Stella discussed the wedding. Grace, having been silent all evening, turned to Stella.

'I'd love to do the wedding photographs', she said hesitantly. 'It would be my gift to you both.'

'I couldn't think of anything better', Stella said smiling. 'Thank you.' She felt as if she had come through an unseen battle, one where the rules were unknown to her.

32

The date of the wedding was planned for a month later. The days passed quickly. Edward was more than solicitous. Frieda was almost childlike in her excitement. Patricia was always at hand. Stella was left with little to do other than to wrap herself in her happiness. She attended to her work but was largely distracted. Angela telephoned every day to discuss the details, outlining any ideas that she had but leaving all the decisions to Stella. Two weeks before the day of the wedding Stella was in her study when the telephone rang. It was Angela.

'Stella, my dear', she said, 'Edward tells me that you have a love of freesias and roses. What do you think about keeping the flower arrangements in the chapel and in the house the same? I thought we could have long stemmed cream freesias and long-stemmed pale pink roses throughout.'

'That sounds wonderful, Angela', she said. 'It sounds perfect.'

'Good', Angela said, a smile in her voice. 'And Edward has also mentioned your insatiable craving for Chinese food. 'Mrs. Dawlish has engaged a young Chinese chef for the day. She said that she was unable to master anything in so short a time!' At this she stopped and burst into laughter. 'She did try Stella. She really did try. You should have seen the devastation in the kitchen. So, she's going to do the "proper food" and there'll be an alternative menu.'

'Thank you, Angela,', Stella said simply. 'You've done so much.'

'No. Thank you, my dear. You've made Magnus and myself very happy. We never believed that this day would arrive. We really had given up all hope.'

When Stella had put down the receiver she went upstairs to her study. She picked up the gold box that Edward had given her. The box that was to house all her good memories. She realized that she would have to take out each memory and fold it even more tightly, to make room for the new ones.

33

Two days before the day of the wedding Edward and Stella left for his parents' house. Patricia, Alex, Lucien and Frieda were to come the following day. Grace was already there. This time when they drove up to the house Stella noted that both Angela and Magnus were there to greet them. Magnus had his arm around his wife.

'Welcome', Angela said, kissing Stella warmly, 'welcome.' She then turned to Edward, putting a hand on his arm. 'Your father's been pacing up and down all morning waiting for you to arrive. He wants to go through the list of wines with you', she laughed. 'He's laid everything out in the wine cellar.'

'It's an important business Angela', he said, 'it's a very important business.' He stepped forward, kissing Stella and shaking Edward by the hand. 'Come in you two. It's freezing out here.'

The house was warm and welcoming. A fire had been lit in the downstairs rooms. The scent of flowers mingled with that of the wood polish. There was the sense of suppressed excitement. Stella marvelled at how she had, at first, thought of this as a cold and dark place.

The following morning after breakfast, Angela went to find Stella and taking her by the hand led her into the drawing room.

'I'd like you to sit here by the fire, Stella. You'll need your rest today. Tomorrow is your big day, and I want you to enjoy every minute of it.'

'There must be something I can do', Stella said. 'Would you like some help in arranging the flowers?'

'Everything's in hand. We'll have lunch when the others arrive from London. Frieda and I will do the flowers this afternoon.' With this she crossed the room to the sideboard. She took out a leather box from one of the drawers and handed it to Stella. 'This is a wedding gift from Magnus and myself. We looked at toasters and washing machines but, in the end, settled on this.'

When Stella opened the leather case, her eyes misted over with tears. Secured against the dark blue velvet base was a necklace of South Sea pearls, their creamy white lustre tinged with gold. As she reached out a finger to touch one of the pearls she felt a teardrop coursing down her cheek. Angela leaned forward to wipe it away.

'Don't cry Stella', she said, trying to hold back her laughter, 'I can always go back and get you the toaster instead. Now you stay here and keep warm. I'll get someone to bring you in some tea in about half an hour.' With that she got up and dropping a kiss on Stella's head, she left the room.

Stella leaned back against the cushions and fell asleep, the case with the pearls left open on her lap. When she awoke, she found Edward sitting beside her, a cup of tea in his hand.

'It's time to get up, my darling', he said. 'The others arrived about an hour ago. We'll be having lunch soon.' He took the leather case from her and put it on the table. 'They're beautiful, aren't they?' he said, lifting the pearls out. 'They belonged to my grandmother.'

'I'll wear them tomorrow, Edward', she said, smiling at him and taking his hand.

The rest of the day passed quickly. Stella spent the afternoon with Patricia in the drawing room, Edward was with his father in the study, Alex and Lucien explored the grounds and Angela and Frieda arranged the flowers in the chapel. Grace, a camera in her hand, moved from room to room going almost unnoticed, her absorption in her work complete. After dinner that evening the men went down to the local pub, Edward saying that he would see Stella the next day. They would not be spending that night together.

On the day of her wedding Stella awoke early. She turned on the bedside lamp. It was a little past five o'clock. She thought about the two people that she would dearly miss that day. She thought about her mother, now long since dead. She thought about Adam and the void that he had left in both

The Unreal Dance

hers and Edward's life. An invitation had been sent to him but there had been no response. Putting on her robe she made her way downstairs, surprised to find that the lights were on in the drawing room. Angela was sitting in an armchair looking through an album of photographs. She looked up when Stella came into the room.

'Sit down, my dear. I'll make you some tea. You must greatly miss the presence of your mother on a day like this', she said perceptively. She kissed Stella on the cheek as she made her way to the kitchen.

At eleven o'clock Stella was ready. The blessing in the chapel was not until eleven thirty. Grace had come into the bedroom several times. She took a photograph of Stella sitting at the dressing table putting on her make-up. She took a photograph of her brushing her hair and tying it into a knot at the nape of her neck. She took one of her bending down to slip on her shoes. She helped Stella into her dress and fastened the pearls in place. She stepped back and looked at Stella.

'You look beautiful', Grace said, 'you really do.' She took one last photograph of Stella standing poised and calm, against a backdrop of an unmade bed and a dressing table cluttered with make-up and a hairbrush. This last photograph would appear in one of her exhibitions.

Stella took one last look in the mirror and made her way downstairs where Magnus was waiting for her. He draped a coat around her shoulders and tucking her arm under his, walked her to the chapel. Here he took the coat from her and placing her hand in the crook of his elbow, he turned to her.

'I wish you every happiness, Stella', he said. 'I wish every happiness for both you and Edward.'

They walked into the chapel to the strains of Handel's Messiah. The light was shining through the stained-glass windows, the colours dancing across the floor. Stella held on tight to Magnus's arm, feeling a momentary sense of foreboding. She felt as if she was watching herself from outside herself. She felt as if she was a guest at someone else's celebrations, an outsider trying to blend in, chameleon like. The moment passed. She let Magnus lead her to where Edward was waiting for her.

The vows that were said were the traditional ones. Edward had said that all he was interested in was that Stella should "honour and obey "him. Stella had smiled at that. He placed the gold ring on Stella's finger. It was the ring with the two hands clasped together. She placed a heavy gold band on his. Father Michael gave them his blessing. As Edward leant forward to kiss Stella there was a loud burst of music. The words of Ben E King's "Stand by Me" rang out throughout the chapel. The guests arose to their feet and clapped. Father Michael shook Edward's hand and smiled at Stella.

'Well Edward', he said, 'I'm ready for a drink and you look as if you could do with one.'

'You're absolutely right, Father,' he laughed, 'let me lead you straight to my father's single malt.'

The guests had filtered out, making their way to the house. Edward and Stella walked slowly back with Patricia, Alex and Lucien. Edward put his arm around Stella's waist and turned to the other three.

'I'd like to introduce you all to my wife, Mrs. Falconer', he said grinning, 'she who has promised to honour and obey me.'

'Good luck with that, Edward', Patricia said, laughing. 'You haven't known her for as long as I have.'

When they reached the house, it was loud with the sound of people talking. Edward, placing a hand protectively on Stella's back, introduced her to his relatives and his parents' friends. Father Michael was talking to Magnus in a quiet corner; each had a large tumbler of whiskey in his hand. Angela was moving from group to group with the excitement of a young girl. Edward went to get a drink for Stella, stopping occasionally to talk to someone. Stella standing alone felt a hand on her arm. When she turned, she saw that it was Adam. She looked at him, her face lighting up.

'Adam', she said quietly, 'I'd given up all hope of you coming. You have no idea how much this means.'

'I wish you well, Stella', he said, smiling at her. 'I wish you both well. You look quite radiant.'

It was then that they became aware of Grace standing beside them, her camera quietly clicking away, a strangely cold look in her eyes.'

'Stella does look radiant, doesn't she?' Grace said. 'Pregnancy will do that to a woman.'

Adam went pale, his jaw tightening, his eyes stricken.
'I didn't realise, Stella', he said, a sadness in his voice. 'I'm happy for you both. If you'll excuse me, I'll go and find Edward.' With that he crossed the room to where Edward was standing talking to Lucien.

Stella looked at Grace, noting an expression of triumph and defiance in the other woman's face, her camera having recorded every movement and every expression of this meeting between Stella and Adam.

Edward did not notice Adam until Adam placed a hand on his shoulder. When he saw who it was, he could barely contain his joy.

'Adam', he said, shaking him by the hand, 'It's been so long. It's been too long.'

'I'm sorry I've come empty handed, Edward. I've been away and only got back this morning. I only had time to change and drive up here.'

'You're being here is more than enough', Edward said warmly. 'I really couldn't ask for anything more.'

'Please Edward. There must be something that I can get you both. It would mean a great deal to me.'

Edward was quiet for a moment.

'There is a rose that Stella wants for the garden, but she hasn't been able to remember the name. It's a rose that you bought for your mother some time ago.'

A shadow seemingly crossed Adam's face.

'The rose is called "Gentle Hermione"', Adam said, the memories of that Sunday at his parents' house flooding back. 'I'll order two. One rose for each of you. I'll have them sent to your house.'

'Why not bring them around yourself?' Edward asked. 'We've missed you. We've missed you more than you can imagine.'

'I'll do that', Adam said gently. 'I'll just say hello to your parents and then I must leave. I have a meeting at the office early this evening.'

Edward watched him walking away. He understood.

Patricia, standing by the window talking to Alex, had witnessed the scene between Stella, Adam and Grace. She had seen Adam's ashen face. She had seen the look of happiness on Stella's face turning to misery when Grace had come up to them. Although she had not heard the words that had passed, she could see the effect that these words had had. She had been wary of Grace from the first. She was even more so now.

By early evening all the guests had left. Patricia, Alex and Lucien would leave the following day. Edward and Stella were to spend a few days at Lucien's house in Dorset, Edward being unable to take time from his work for what he called a "proper honeymoon". This, he had promised Stella, would come after his exhibition.

The next morning after the others had left Edward and Stella sat with his parents in the drawing room. The fire had been lit, and a tray of tea had been brought in.

'I can't thank you both enough', Stella said to Angela and Magnus. 'You have given us a day to be remembered.'

'The pleasure was all ours', Angela said taking Stella's hand. 'It's been too long since the house had such life breathed into it. And', she continued, 'I think that you'll find that Mrs. Dawlish has packed your car with more than enough food for a month. Call us when you get back. Magnus and I were thinking of coming to London for a few days. We'll stay at the Reform Club and see you both when you have time.'

34

After they had returned from their few days in Dorset, Edward and Stella's life settled into a routine. Edward would arise around dawn and go up to his studio to work. There were days when Stella did not see him until the evening. Stella would work in her study in the mornings and attend meetings in the afternoon. This routine was not much different to before they had got married, except that Edward had to work longer hours to make up for the days lost.

One evening, about ten days after they had returned, there was a telephone call from Grace. She had compiled the album of photographs that she had taken at the time of the wedding and wondered when she could bring it over. She suggested that she could perhaps come over for dinner later that week. It was arranged that she would come the following evening. Stella had been left with little choice.

The next day Stella spent the morning working in her study, going out after lunch to do the shopping for that evening's dinner. Edward had said that he would be down around six o'clock. That way they could spend an hour or so together before Grace arrived.

It was mid-afternoon when Stella returned to the house. She unpacked the shopping and made herself a cup of tea. She had been filled with a sense of dread all day. She was afraid of seeing the photographs that Grace had taken. She was afraid of the ones that had been taken of her and Adam. Grace's work had a way of revealing what was best left hidden. Of seeing things that were best left unseen.

Stella went upstairs to take a shower before coming down to start preparing the meal. The house was warm, yet she could feel herself shivering. When

Edward came down Stella was in the kitchen slicing a large bunch of spring onions. They were to have pan-fried fillets of sea bass on a bed of stir-fried green beans and spiced noodles. It was a meal that would be prepared when Grace arrived. Edward poured himself a drink and kissing Stella on the nape of the neck, sat down at the kitchen table. He loved to watch her when she was cooking. There was a total absorption in what she was doing. She turned and smiled at him, thinking how tired he looked. There were only a few months left before his exhibition, and he had to make up for the time that had been lost. When he spoke, it was as if he had been reading her mind.

'Another week or so', he told her, 'And I'll have caught up with the days that I've missed. After that I'm going to try and take a whole day off each week. We've spent so little time together recently. I find myself missing you.'

'There'll be plenty of time after the exhibition', Stella said, 'there'll be plenty of time.'

The doorbell rang. Edward went to let Grace in. Stella stiffened, her knuckles white over the knife that she was holding. She could hear Edward talking to Grace in the hallway and then showing her into the sitting room. She could hear ice being put into a glass and a drink being poured. She wiped her hands and went in to join them.

'Hallo Grace,' she said, noting the large package on the table, 'how are you?'

'I'm well Stella', Grace replied. 'I hope you like the photographs that I've taken. There are some wonderful ones of you.' She got up and handed the wrapped package to Stella. She noted that Stella hesitated for a moment before opening it.

Stella carefully took the paper off. Inside was not the album of photographs that she had been expecting but a beautifully bound book. All the photographs were in black and white with a tinge of sepia. Each evoked vivid memories of that given moment. There was one that Stella was particularly drawn to. She kept going back to it again and again. It was one of Edward and her taking a walk near the woods. She had her hand on Edward's shoulder. She was steadying herself as he knelt down to remove a stone that had lodged in her shoe. She could clearly remember that day. She he could clearly remember the conversations that they had had. This was not just a collection of photographs. It was the story of a deep love between two people. Stella raised her eyes and smiled at Grace.

'Thank you, Grace,', she said, with warmth in her voice, 'thank you.' She handed the book to Edward and went into the kitchen to prepare the dinner.

After that night Grace came to the house often. She brought with her the more traditional wedding photographs that she had taken. These were in colour. One day she brought with her a copy of the photograph that she had seen Stella looking at again and again. The one with Edward and Stella walking near the woods. She had had this framed. Stella put it on the wall in her study. A cautious friendship developed between the two women, the past never spoken of.

35

The months before Edward's exhibition passed quickly. Stella and Edward spent Christmas with Edward's parents. Grace had gone to stay with friends in Scotland. She had been commissioned to take photographs of highland villages. It was in the New Year when they saw Adam again. He arrived on their doorstep one evening, carrying two large rose bushes. When he had handed these to a delighted Edward, he went back to the car and brought back with him two slate grey pots.

'These roses do well in pots', he explained to Edward. 'It also means that you can move them around until you find them a place that suits you.'

Edward burst out laughing.

'Have you ever thought about doing a gardening programme, Adam?' he said. 'I never realized that you knew so much about plants.'

Stella hearing the laughter coming from the hallway went to see what was going on. She had not expected to see Adam there. 'Adam', she said, smiling at him, 'what on earth are these?' She pointed to the plants, one under each arm.

'These, Stella', he replied, 'are your wedding present. Two matching "Gentle Hermione" rose bushes. I hope you're not going to mock me as Edward has.'

'Of course not', she laughed. 'I insist that you stay for dinner. It'll be in about half an hour.'

When she went back into the kitchen, Stella could not stop smiling. They had not seen or heard from Adam since the day of the wedding. He had obviously needed time to come to terms with everything. Now he was back in their lives.

February had passed and March had arrived. It was two weeks to Edward's exhibition. Each day a large van would arrive. Two men would go up to Edward's studio to wrap the paintings to take to the gallery. The sculptures were carried from the studio at the bottom of the garden. Edward was there to oversee all this. It was over eighteen months of work. Stella wondered what would have happened if she had not met him at that first exhibition. If Adam had been abroad, as he often was, it might have been a long time before they would have come across each other. She might have by that time been married to Adam. She wondered what would have happened then. Stella placed her hands protectively over her stomach. The baby was due in the last week of June. It had been a year of great surprises.

On the day of the exhibition Edward left for the gallery straight after breakfast. He would be there all day. Patricia was coming to the house mid-morning. They were going to look around the shops and have lunch. Angela and Magnus had come to London the day before and were staying at their club. They were all to have dinner after the exhibition. Edward had said that he would be back in the late afternoon and that they would be going to the gallery together. Stella went up to the dressing room to put out the clothes that she would be wearing that night. She showered and dressed, going downstairs to wait for Patricia.

Patricia arrived at eleven o'clock. They went out straight after that. They looked around the shops not buying anything and settled down to a long leisurely lunch. They went back to the house mid-afternoon. Edward returned just before six o'clock to shower and change. They left shortly after. When they arrived at the gallery it was already full. Ursula, Edward's agent, was standing near the entrance deep in conversation with a group of people. She raised a hand in a silent greeting to Stella and Edward. They walked over to her.

'Is that a new Chanel suit that you're wearing, Ursula?' Edward asked her.

'Yes', Ursula replied, grinning broadly, 'and I'm going to buy a couple more tomorrow. Almost two thirds of the works are already sold.'

'Shame on you woman', he said smiling. 'With the fees that you take my poor wife will have to spend the rest of her days in nylon smocks and my poor child will go hungry.'

Stella was still laughing when she went over to where Angela and Magnus were standing.

'Isn't this marvellous, Stella?' Magnus said, with great pride in his voice. 'You must be very proud.'

'I'm afraid that my only contribution to all this', Stella said, gesturing toward the paintings, 'was making sure that Edward got enough to eat.'

'I'm sure, my dear', Magnus said to her solemnly, 'that you realize that it's a great deal more than that. The bleakness and the torment of his earlier works are almost faded.'

Angela, standing by silently, put her hand on Stella's arm.

'You should go and talk to the other guests, Stella', she said gently. 'After all, you're one of the stars of this show. We'll see you later.'

Stella went from room to room, looking at the paintings and the sculptures. Although she was familiar with all these works, they looked more imposing in the setting of the gallery. She was about to go and join Edward when she noticed a small side room. A crowd was gathered here. There was only one painting in this room, a single light shining upon it. The painting was of a mother with her infant child. She was looking into the distance, holding the child protectively to her breast. Stella had not seen this work before. There was a serenity about the woman's face, a grace and a purity. The work was titled "Birth and Rebirth". Stella stood looking at the painting for a long, long time. She was unaware that Edward was standing at the back of the room watching her.

A week later, after they had returned from lunch, Edward took Stella's hand and led her to her study. Stella gasped. The painting of the mother and her child was hanging on the wall, the sunlight through the windows lighting it up. Stella looking at it felt a tear slide down her cheek.

The Unreal Dance

'I don't blame you for crying', Edward said. 'You should have seen my tears when Ursula made me pay the full price for it. Not even a staff discount. She said that she could have sold it again and again for double the price. That woman shows no mercy.'

'Well,', said Stella laughing, 'she did tell me that she was looking for a new car.'

Later that evening while they were having dinner, Edward reached out and took Stella's hand in his.

'What about that honeymoon I promised you, Stella?' he asked. 'Where would you like to go?'

Stella was silent for a moment.

'Would you mind very much if we didn't go anywhere?' she said. 'The baby is due in three months, and I'd like to enjoy every minute of the wait.'

'That's fine by me, Stella. But don't forget that there'll be another baby and another baby. I want a whole brood. The honeymoon might be a long time coming.'

'I can wait, Edward', she said smiling, 'I can wait.'

The last week of June arrived, and Stella had still not gone into labour. The baby was ten days overdue. Edward was getting impatient. He had cleared the bedroom next to theirs for the nursery. He had painted it and put up shelves. He had collected his old cot from his parents' house. Frieda had engaged her niece Ella, who was a trained nanny, to come and work full time. Everything was ready.

'Have you talked to Dr. Feingold? Edward asked, with some anxiety in his voice. 'Does he know when the baby might come?'

'Yes, I have talked to him', Stella replied patiently, 'and he said that the baby would come when it was ready.'

Two days later the baby was ready.

Edward had intended to be present at the birth of the child but the fear and anxiety in his eyes made Stella nervous. He stood holding on to a chair looking pale and faint. The nurse suggested that he should wait outside and when Edward looked at Stella, he saw her nod her agreement.

He found Patricia and Alex waiting in the corridor. Patricia handed him a cup of strong coffee and Alex handed him a silver hip flask of whiskey. It was almost twelve hours later that he heard a baby's cry coming from Stella's room. The nurse opened the door and asked him to come in. Stella, now exhausted, was lying back against the pillows. He saw that she was smiling. The nurse placed the baby in Edward's arms. She told him that it was a girl. Stella watched Edward looking down at his daughter. She saw that from that first moment he was lost, completely lost.

'Should I be jealous, Edward?' Stella said laughing. 'Should I be really jealous?'

'Oh yes Stella, you should. You really should.'

After long moments of looking down on the baby's face, he looked at Stella.

'Beatrice', he said quietly. 'What do you think of the name Beatrice, my darling?'

'It's a beautiful name', Stella said, 'quite beautiful.'

Edward was always to refer to the child as his Bumble Bea.

Angela came to visit Stella the next day. Grace had been there for most of the morning, moving around quietly taking photographs. She had left by the time that Angela arrived.

'Magnus will be coming later', Angela said, unable to take her eyes off the child. 'He's out celebrating with Edward. I just hope that the pair of them will be sober enough not to go to the wrong hospital.' She placed a finger on the baby's cheek, stroking it softly. 'My Beatrice', she said to herself, her eyes misting over, 'my little Beatrice.'

Stella lay back against the pillows silently watching the two of them. She knew that this child would be well loved.

'I've had flowers delivered to the house', Angela said, taking a beautifully wrapped package from her handbag, 'but I wanted to give you this myself.'

Stella carefully took off the wrapping paper. Inside was a book. It was a first edition of A.A. Milne's Winnie the Pooh, the dark green cover well-worn and the pages well thumbed.

'It's been in our family since it was first published', Angela said, 'and now it belongs to Beatrice.'

'Thank you, Angela', Stella said. ''Your kindness toward me has been immeasurable.'

'It is I who should thank you, Stella', Angela said, leaning over to kiss her cheek. 'It is I who should thank you. Before Edward met you our family was fractured, broken even. And now there is a future.'

Stella would always remember these words.

ACT III
TRAGEDY AND DEATH

36

It was the day of Beatrice's fourth birthday. Edward had insisted on a party. He had said that he would take charge of this. There were to be about twenty children. There was to be clown, a magician and a puppet show. Frieda had spent all week making cakes and jellies. Edward had spent all morning blowing up balloons. Grace was to take the photographs. He was almost as excited as Beatrice.

Patricia and Alex arrived at midday, Alex carrying two bottles of chilled champagne and Patricia an expensively wrapped box.

'My daughter's too young to drink', Edward laughed, taking the bottles from Alex. 'You should know better.' He took them through to where Stella was laying out plates and folding napkins. He got four glasses and opened one of the bottles. Before he had time to pour out the champagne, Patricia put a hand on his arm.

'Alex and I are getting married', she said. 'He forced me into accepting.'

Stella burst out laughing and clapped her hands together.

'I can't imagine anyone forcing you to do anything, Patricia', she said. 'When is the great event to take place?'

'I wanted to wait a couple of years', Alex said, looking at Patricia, 'but she said that she couldn't wait more than six weeks. So that's when it's going to be.'

Edward filled their glasses and a toast was made. Patricia handed Stella the box that she had brought with her.

'This is for Beatrice', she said to Stella, 'but I'd like you to open it.'

Stella opened the box. Inside was a dress for Beatrice. The silk velvet was of a deep violet colour, the collar and cuffs in cream lace. For years to come the details of this dress would stay in Stella's mind, like a still photograph that would be taken out to be looked at again and again. She took the dress upstairs and asked Ella to put it on Beatrice when she had finished bathing her. When she went downstairs Grace had arrived and was already moving through the downstairs rooms taking photographs. She took ones of Frieda working in the kitchen, she took ones of the empty sitting room with balloons hanging down, she took ones of Edward talking to Patricia and Alex. Stella had long ago realized that Grace's work was not about instances in isolation. The images made up a story, a story with a beginning and an end. A story that would capture what had come before and what had come after, the images in between holding the whole together.

37

Six weeks later, the day before Patricia and Alex's wedding, Edward and Stella were in the courtyard in front of the house packing up the car. It was a long drive, and they had decided to start out early. Frieda was to stay at the house to look after Beatrice. Ella would come in every day to help. Edward and Stella were to spend that night and the night of the wedding with Patricia's parents. After that they were to spend two nights in a hotel in north Devon. Edward had said that it would be the honeymoon that they had never had. Stella had laughed and said that it was his way of economizing. They were in the car ready to drive off. Beatrice and Frieda were on the front doorstep waving them off. Edward suddenly opened the car door and got out of the car. He went up to Beatrice and picking her up, held on to her tightly.

'We'll be back soon Bumble Bea', he said, putting his forehead against hers. 'I want you to look after Frieda and make sure that she doesn't stay up too long every night.'

Stella could hear the child giggling and saying that she would make sure that Frieda went to bed early every night. This was another still photograph, another still image in Stella's mind. But this image was one that was one that was in isolation, with nothing to say what had gone before and what was to come after. Not all stories have a clear beginning and a clear ending. There are often times when the truth is obscured and distorted.

The wedding was a small affair. Patricia and Alex drove back to London the day after. They were going from there to Rome for their honeymoon. Edward and Stella drove to the hotel in Devon. It was a small hotel with only a dozen rooms. They took long walks during the day, eating in the small dining room in the evenings. Afterwards they would sit in front of the open fire in the lounge area and talk. They called the house several times a day to check on Beatrice. When they left the hotel to return to London Edward chose a longer route, one that would take them through small villages and towns. They had told Frieda that they would be home around eight o'clock. When they were an hour away from home Edward suggested that they should stop at a pub that he knew, for supper. He would call Frieda and tell her that they would be home later than planned. After the meal was finished and the coffee brought Edward went outside to call the house. There was little signal in the pub. There was no answer on the landline of the house, so Edward called Frieda's mobile telephone. This she always kept with her. She answered on the second ring.

'Frieda', Edward said, 'is everything all right? I called on the house telephone, but you obviously didn't hear it.'

'I'm not at the house, Edward', Frieda replied. 'Grace came around this afternoon and said that she would stay with Beatrice until you returned tonight. She sent me home.'

Edward was silent for a moment.

'Thank you, Frieda,', he said, 'we' re on our way home now. I'll see you in the morning.'

Edward then tried to ring Grace on her mobile telephone. It did not ring. It went straight through to her voicemail.

When Edward went back into the pub Stella looked up at him. She was smiling.

'Is everything all right?' she asked, 'Is Beatrice in bed?'

'I don't know, ' he replied quietly. 'Grace arrived at the house this afternoon saying that she would look after Beatrice until we returned. She sent Frieda home. I tried Grace's number, but it seems to be switched off. They're probably both asleep.'

The drive home was a silent one, Edward driving faster than he normally would. When they arrived back at the house it was a little past ten o'clock. All the lights were on. They left themselves in quietly thinking that perhaps Grace had fallen asleep in the sitting room. She was not there. Edward, with

Stella following, then took the stairs up to Beatrice's room. A single lamp lit the room. Beatrice was lying on her back dressed in the velvet dress that Patricia had given her. Her arms were folded across her stomach, her small feet bare. Grace was lying on her side facing the child. It was then that they noted the bottle of vodka, now half empty, on the table beside Grace. There was a smaller pill bottle beside that of the vodka. That was empty. Edward crossed the room to where Beatrice was lying. He tried to wake her, but her hand was limp, her body cold. He looked up at Stella, a desolation and a despair in his eyes. Stella looked back at him, unable to move. It was at this moment that Grace half opened her eyes and stared into those of Edward's. She put out her hand toward Edward. They were never to know whether it was to ask for help or for forgiveness. Stella took a step forward to see if she could help Grace, but Edward gestured her not to do so. They sat in silence for several hours, until they were sure that all breath had left Grace's body.

It was then that Stella went over to where Beatrice was lying and laid her head on the child's breast. The cry that she let out was not human in sound, her body wracked by uncontrollable sobs. Edward did not try to comfort Stella. He was isolated in his own grief. Their child was dead, their love for each other poisoned at the roots.

38

Beatrice's funeral was held ten days later. She was to be buried in the grounds by the family chapel. Grace was to be buried in the local graveyard the following week. Patricia and Alex had returned early from their honeymoon. Adam and Lucien had driven up from London.

The service that was held was a subdued one. Father Michael looking at the small coffin beside him, almost unable to speak. The day outside that had started as grey and overcast had turned to bright sunshine.

Stella, dry eyed, stood beside Edward and watched the coffin being lowered into the ground. It was then that she looked up and stared into Angela's eyes. It was in that instant that she realised, with a certainty that brooked no doubt, that Angela had known what had gone on before and what might come after. Stella looked away.

EPILOGUE

It was late afternoon. Stella stood by the window of her flat looking out to the sea. There was an almost imperceptible line separating the grey of the sky from the grey of the water. But Stella did not see this. What she saw was a large dance hall. She was alone at the centre of this, the other dancers having long left. She was slowly moving around, dancing the ghost dance. The dance danced without a partner. It was then that she became aware of the sound of a voice, a voice that was getting louder and louder. It was a moment before she realized that it was the sound of her own voice, whispering out aloud the words of a long-forgotten nursery rhyme from her childhood-----

Ladybird, ladybird, fly away home,
Your house is on fire, your children all gone.

For Jill Dawson …without whose guidance and wisdom I would not have got past page one. Thank you.

Printed in Dunstable, United Kingdom